"Sydney, honey, we're an item now. All we have to do is act like it," Zinn teased

"A little kissing, hugging, mugging for the paparazzi outside the Hard Rock Cafe," he continued. "No big deal."

Sydney glared at Zinn.

"What's the matter, babe?"

"Zinn, why do I feel like you're taking advantage of the situation?"

His face was the picture of innocence. "I don't know why, do you?"

"Because I think you actually like the idea."

He grinned. "What am I supposed to do, hate the prospect of kissing you? As I recall, it wasn't so bad the other night when we were doing it naturally."

Sydney flushed. "You *are* taking advantage. But remember, it's just an act."

Zinn gave her a provocative look. "Well, I can't promise I won't enjoy it."

Janice Kaiser is renowned for her highly emotional, bestselling Superromance novels. A long-time avid fan of Temptation, Janice decided to try her hand at writing a Temptation story—and we're glad she did! The heroine of *Heartthrob* is Sydney Charles, a private eye with a smart mouth and warm heart whose beat is the glitzy streets of Hollywood. Like Sydney, even though we may all sometimes make fun of the phony aspects of Hollywood, we still love to watch movies and swoon at heartthrobs. Watch for Janice's next Temptation, *The Maverick*, part of the Rebels & Rogues miniseries, coming in November 1992.

Books by Janice Kaiser

HARLEQUIN SUPERROMANCE
242–LOVE CHILD
256–CHANCES
287–STOLEN MOMENTS
403–BODY AND SOUL
494–THE BIG SECRET

Heartthrob
JANICE KAISER

Harlequin Books

TORONTO • NEW YORK • LONDON
AMSTERDAM • PARIS • SYDNEY • HAMBURG
STOCKHOLM • ATHENS • TOKYO • MILAN
MADRID • WARSAW • BUDAPEST • AUCKLAND

For Stacey and Melissa Krum

Published August 1992

ISBN 0-373-25506-3

HEARTTHROB

Printed in U.S.A.

1

"FORGIVE A STUPID question," Abe Cohen said, "but how do you propose to protect somebody you feel nothing for but contempt?"

Sydney Charles shifted uncomfortably in her chair, warning herself to watch her mouth. The last thing she could afford to do was alienate Abe Cohen. He was the key to getting the job. "Mr. Cohen . . ." she began in a measured tone.

"It's Abe, doll. Your mama's called me Abe for thirty years. You can, too."

"Abe," Sydney said, trying to act a good deal calmer than she felt, "a cop doesn't have to love a murder victim to track down his killer, and a security specialist doesn't have to be devoted to her employer to protect him. Anyway, my understanding is I would be protecting Zinn Garrett's little girl, not him. As far as I'm concerned, the fact that he's an actor would be incidental to the job. Considering that he signs the checks, I'll find a way to be polite to him."

"'Polite' isn't the issue," Cohen replied, chomping down on his cigar. "Stars have egos, they've got sensitivities. They're used to people kissing their hand. You know that. Now, Zinn's not bad as far as most of them go—at times he can be a pretty down-to-earth guy—but he's part of the system. He's got the salary, the adoration, and he lives in this town. More important than anything, he adores his kid. Need I say more?"

Sydney gave her long blond braid an impatient tug and tossed it over her shoulder. "No. I hear you loud and clear, Abe. I was just being up front with you about *my feelings* toward actors." She lowered her voice, sounding as though she was imparting a confidence. "I'm not a groupie. I know Hollywood well, and I don't particularly like the people. Present company excluded, of course," she quickly added.

Abe Cohen smiled wanly, then leaned back in his big black desk-chair to reflect on the situation.

Sydney thought he looked as if he could have been in the movies himself—as a character actor, of course. He was well into his sixties, had a bulbous nose and a face with the wrinkles of a Sharpei. His stomach protruded over his trousers, stretching his shirt as taut as the skin of a sausage. He had a shiny bald pate, and the inevitable cigar was jammed in one corner of his mouth, like a pacifier.

His office, located in an older building in downtown Beverly Hills, wasn't sumptuous, but it was very comfortable and was filled with Hollywood mementos. Sydney's mother had told her he even had an Oscar that had been willed to him by a deceased client. The paneled walls of his office were covered with photographs of dozens of film stars, past and present—most of them in his company, naturally.

Soon after she had arrived that morning, Abe had pointed to a picture of himself standing between her mother, Lee Lorraine—who looked remarkably beautiful, dressed in short shorts, heels and a halter top—and her darkly handsome father, Dick Charles. It had been taken on a movie lot twenty-seven years earlier. Sydney had never seen that particular photograph before, but she didn't dwell on it for long. Still, occasionally during the conversation her gaze was drawn back to the picture of the father she'd hardly known.

Suddenly Abe Cohen leaned forward over his desk. "Here's my problem, Sydney. If I'm to recommend you to Zinn Garrett, I need more than just the fact that I know your ma. Give me a reason. I have people pitching projects at me all the time. You wouldn't believe the razzmatazz I hear, sitting in this chair. So let's hear your pitch. Why *should* I recommend you?" He blew a puff of smoke toward the ceiling and leaned back again.

Sydney knew this was the time to do her song-and-dance routine. She had opened her own shop as a private investigator a few months before, and business wasn't going well. All she'd gotten so far was a couple of small insurance-fraud investigations. So, she'd decided to look for contracts as a security specialist—the kind of work she'd done for her previous employer.

The sad truth was, she was desperate. Her savings had finally run out and she'd been forced to give up her apartment, swallow her pride and move back in with her mother. Worse, if she didn't nail down a big job soon, she'd have to throw in the towel and go to work in someone else's shop. Her best hope of finding something was in the area of threat evaluation and personal security. Protecting people paid well, and it could give her the exposure she needed.

"I'll be frank with you, Abe. I'm not the Michelle Pfeiffer of private investigators. I'm not a superstar, yet. But I'm damned good at what I do. And I've got a track record. I did a lot of personal security work when I was with Candy Gonzalez, and I did it well. Now that I'm on my own, I plan to make it one of my specialties."

"How long did you work for this guy Gonzalez?"

"A little over a year."

"And before that?"

Sydney gritted her teeth, determined not to falter. "Before that I was at UCLA. I majored in criminology."

Cohen tapped the ashes from his cigar into an ashtray. "Point is, you don't exactly have a track record a mile long."

Sydney looked out the window at the palm trees. Then she shook her head. "I may not have three Oscar nominations on my résumé, but my first film was a success. I've proven I can do it."

"Well, to continue the metaphor, doll, the producer in question has put all his marbles on this project. Question is whether he's willing to gamble on a new starlet, or does he go with the sure box-office draw."

Sydney leaned forward. "I can do it. All I need is a chance."

Abe Cohen waved at her with his cigar hand. "Honey, let me give you some advice. In this town, needing something is a killer. There can't even be a hint of desperation on your face. Take your ma, for example. During her low period she was eating soup made of ham bones and borrowing a week's rent at a time. But when she went to the studio, she could have been a millionaire, a star. If you looked close you could tell the dress wasn't new, but she had success written all over her."

Sydney looked down at her hands. "My mother was an actress. I'm not."

"Zinn Garrett is an actor, though. And image and attitude just happen to be a little more important in Hollywood than in Des Moines."

Sydney sat up straight in her chair. "I'm not going to beg, Mr. Cohen. I can handle the job, and I can handle Zinn Garrett. I have no doubt about that."

He sighed. "Well, to be honest, I'd rather be sending you to MGM than to do battle with that maniac who's trying to get Zinn's kid. But it's your decision, not mine."

Sydney's heart skipped a beat. "Then you're going to recommend me?"

"Yes. But that's the best I can do. The rest will be up to you."

Sydney slapped the desk happily with the palm of her hand. "That's terrific!"

"Don't figure that means you've got the job. Same as with my actors, all I can do is open doors. This is a selling town, honey. You'll have to sell *him*."

Sydney couldn't help beaming. It was as though the fog had lifted and there it was—a rainbow right up over the Hollywood hills. The kidnapping threat to Zinn Garrett's little girl had been in all the papers. It was big. Real big. And it could make her career.

Abe Cohen watched her with apparent amusement. "You know, I was surprised you never got the movie bug yourself, kiddo. Your ma and I talked about it years ago. She wanted me to have a word with you. Bet she never told you that. I said to her, 'Lee, you can lead a horse to water, but that's it. If they don't have fire in the gut for movies, they don't got a prayer.'"

It was a subject Sydney had heard about often while growing up. And, until she was old enough to stand on her hind legs and resist, she'd dutifully gone to every casting call for child actresses the studios announced. It had been both her mother's avocation and dream to see her daughter a star. Sydney sometimes wondered if her lack of interest in films hadn't been an even bigger disappointment to her mother than Lee's own failed career.

"You got the face and figure for it," Abe said, letting his gaze skitter down to the scoop of her white cotton sundress and as far below as the desk would allow. "But I guess it wasn't enough that it was in the genes on both sides."

Sydney unconsciously pulled on her braid. People often said she was the image of her mother as a young woman. But in every other way they couldn't have been more different. "No," she replied. "Acting is not my thing."

Abe nodded sadly again. "I suppose your ma told you that I used to represent your old man."

Sydney felt an all-too-familiar pain gnaw at her, so she smiled to cover it up. Dick Charles was the last person on earth she wanted to talk about, but she'd known it would be unavoidable. "Yes, Mother has mentioned it," she admitted, hoping that Abe would drop the topic.

"Dick was one of the lions," he said, plunging ahead without noticing her tone. He chewed on the cigar. "A lion when we still had lions in this business." Then Abe stared off—the way her mother sometimes did when she was remembering.

Sydney gritted her teeth but held her silence. The very least she could do, now that Abe had promised to recommend her to Garrett, was to be gracious.

"It's a shame you didn't know your old man better," Abe said.

Sydney swallowed hard. "I had my mother. She gave me a happy childhood. That's what counts."

He smiled and nodded. "You know, kid, you remind me a hell of a lot of your ma."

"Thanks. I take that as a compliment."

He beamed approvingly. "So, how is Lee? She sounded good when I talked to her on the phone."

"Fine. Arthritis slows her up quite a bit, but she's okay."

"Arthritis can be hell." He grinned again. "Especially for a dancer, like your ma."

Sydney scoffed. "Mother hasn't danced for years."

Abe Cohen stabbed at the air with his cigar. "Not professionally, maybe, but she's danced. It's in the blood, honey. A hoofer never quits, even if it's only a little two-step on the living-room rug.

"Yeah, her career was one of the great tragedies of Hollywood. Maybe came on the scene a little late. Timing is everything in this business, you know. If anyone deserved to make it but didn't, it was Lee Lorraine. You hear that a lot from the old-timers around town."

Sydney shifted uncomfortably in her finely upholstered chair. It was hard, listening to how her mother never quite made it, and her father had—especially when her mother had been a devoted parent and her father... Well, he'd been less than admirable, to say the least.

"Performers like your ma, they're a dying breed. *We're* a dying breed, I should say."

Sydney could tell the crusty old huckster liked to play with people. Self-deprecation was undoubtedly one of his tricks. But the main thing was that he was willing to help her get her foot in the door with Zinn Garrett. For that she was grateful.

Now that she'd gained his cooperation, she was eager to get going. "So, what happens now, Abe?"

"I told Zinn you'd be at his place at one o'clock." He handed her a slip of paper with the address.

Sydney couldn't keep the surprise out of her voice. "You mean you already made the appointment?"

"Yes, but if I didn't like what I saw, I'd have called him to cancel. When I talked to him yesterday, he was ready to hire somebody else. I knew next week would be too late."

"Thank you," she said, unable to keep the excitement out of her voice. She jumped to her feet, reached across the desk and shook his hand.

"Break a leg, kid."

Sydney headed toward the door, trying to contain the bounce in her step.

"By the way," Abe said, stopping her. "Zinn's got an eye for a set of gams. That figure of yours won't hurt." He took in her shapely calves and nicely turned ankles, then winked. "A word to the wise."

Sydney nodded and turned to the door, feeling as if a little air had just been let out of her balloon. That was one thing about Hollywood that she'd never liked: The women were always selling themselves, and the men, too, for that matter. Not always sexually, but that was sometimes a natural part of it, like the makeup and the clothes. Seeing what had happened to her mother had turned her against that way of life.

"Thanks, Abe."

When she reached her Honda hatchback in the parking lot, she noticed a pool of oil under the engine and big black drops plopping into it. Sydney groaned. The motor had been sounding strange for days. Her car simply couldn't give out on her in addition to everything else! She'd have to find a gas station and get more oil, then hope she could get to Zinn Garrett's place in Pacific Palisades and back to her mother's house in Glendale. She looked at her watch. She'd have to hurry if she was going to make it.

Sydney got in the car. Fortunately it started.

SYDNEY TOYED NERVOUSLY with her braid as she waited in her Honda on Las Miradas Drive. She had arrived a few moments late, but Zinn Garrett wasn't at home. She had spoken with the housekeeper on the intercom at the gate, and had been asked to wait outside. Paranoia was running high—which, she decided, was good under the circumstances.

Another ten minutes had passed, and Garrett still hadn't shown up. Staring at the closed security gate, Sydney prayed that he hadn't made other arrangements. After all she and her mother had gone through to get Abe Cohen's help, that would be the last straw.

Sydney was absolutely determined to make it as a private investigator. The excitement of the chase, the problem solving, even the occasional danger appealed to her. True, a lot of the work was routine and sheer drudgery, but there were payoffs, and that's what she lived for.

There was no question she'd rather be on a robbery stakeout, or walking into the den of a drug dealer, wired with listening devices—anything but sweet-talking a narcissistic film star and groveling at the altar of his ego. But at least she understood the Hollywood mentality and knew what to expect. Besides, with any luck, Zinn Garrett would be off shooting most of the time, leaving his daughter in her care. The first order of business, though, was to land the job.

Sighing wearily, Sydney looked out at the view that extended from the Pacific to the high rises of downtown Beverly Hills. Zinn Garrett's house sat on the very top of a hill, affording a spectacular vista of the entire basin. At the moment the vista was bathed in filmy smog, rendering the distant L.A. skyline nearly invisible.

The house itself was fairly new, possibly built by Garrett himself. It was Mediterranean in style, but instead of the usual pinkish beige with a red-tiled roof, the house was sparkling white and the roof was covered with aqua tiles. The sweeping lawn was studded with royal palms. Next to the house were beds planted with flowering shrubs.

Sydney looked at her watch again. Garrett was over half an hour late. Not a good omen. During the drive from Abe's office, she'd given herself a pep talk, but now she was having doubts. Maybe she *was* desperate—too desperate to hide it.

The day before, when she had moved everything back to her mother's place, she'd felt like such a failure. It had nearly broken her heart when Lee had offered to take a few students on in order to bring in a little more money.

Her mother had supported them between films by running a dance studio for aspiring child stars and would-be chorus girls. It had been a modest living, but it kept her within dreaming range of the business she so dearly loved—until age and arthritis had crept up on her.

Sydney recognized that her mother had never completely let go of her dreams; she had simply transferred her ambition to Sydney, talking movies to her from the day she had been born until she went off to college. Not that the talk did any good. Sydney had a mind of her own and, as her mother had often said, the mouth to go with it.

Their conflict over the issue hadn't been easy for either of them. Sydney had often agonized, growing up. She loved her mother dearly, and was grateful for her many sacrifices. Still, she couldn't support Lee's mindless devotion to the business that had betrayed her, and brought them both so much unhappiness.

But whenever Sydney tried to express her dislike for the movie business, her mother would get furious. "If it weren't for films, you'd never have been born," she'd say. "I don't regret what happened between your father and me for a minute. We were blessed with a beautiful child."

Of course, she never added, "Even if you were illegitimate, even if you never saw your father except on the screen, even if he treated us both like we were lepers." Those were the thoughts that Sydney harbored, the thoughts that sustained her resentment of Dick Charles, actors, and everything they stood for.

But that was all old stuff now. Her father had died a legend; and she and her mother were little more than footnotes in his glossy biographies. At least his money had ended up providing Lee with a free-and-clear house—some measure of security for her old age.

As for her mother taking on students again when she could barely walk, Sydney would have none of that. She'd get a job serving hamburgers at McDonald's first.

Adjusting her sunglasses, she glanced into the side mirror. There was still no sign of any vehicle. Was she going to be stood up by Garrett?

Impatiently Sydney got out of the car, flipping her braid over her shoulder as she leaned against the fender, and glanced down the street in the direction he would have to come. She smoothed the front of her dress. Its hem was well above her knees and the neckline was low enough to reveal a little cleavage. Usually she preferred pants for working, but her mother had insisted that sex appeal was essential in Hollywood. Sydney didn't like the idea, but she deferred to her mother's familiarity with how egotistical stars were likely to think.

The sun blazed brightly. There was no breeze and it was hot. She remembered her very first assignment as a P.I. soon after she went to work for Candy Gonzalez. It had been a hot July day, not much different from this one. She had been so nervous she could hardly drive. Her assignment was to dig up some background information on a man who'd been writing crank letters to their client, an outfielder with the Los Angeles Dodgers. It had been her first taste of threat evaluation.

Working for Candy had given her the experience she needed, but investigators were an independent lot by nature. And Sydney wanted to be her own boss in the worst way. The question now was whether she'd jumped the gun because of her impatience.

She folded her arms under her breasts and ran her practiced eye over the gate and high wall surrounding Garrett's property. The wall was obviously designed to turn away the curious, the stargazers, the tourists. But it wasn't much of a deterrent to someone determined to get inside.

Sydney would tell Garrett that when they met—demonstrate her professionalism any way she could. To give herself some hope of getting the job, she'd have to dispel his doubts right up front.

Just as she glanced at her watch again, she heard a car coming up the street. A flash of sunlight reflected off the windshield; she saw the sheen of silver paint and chrome. It was a Jaguar sedan, and it was moving fast. She figured it was Garrett.

Her stomach muscles tightened as she stood upright. The car slowed, finally stopping across the street at the gate she'd been watching. The driver looked her way momentarily, then punched his code into the automatic security panel, and the gate swung open.

Sydney got her purse from the car and started walking across the street. Before she reached the gate, it closed. The Jaguar moved on up the long drive to the house and the man behind the wheel got out. He turned and looked toward her, seeming to hesitate for a moment.

"Mr. Garrett!" she called.

He put his hands on his hips as though he were undecided, then began sauntering back down the drive. The sunlight reflected off his pure white shirt. Even though he had on large dark sunglasses, Sydney could tell that it was in fact Zinn Garrett.

His face was familiar, though even more handsome in real life than on the screen. Garrett had done a few not terribly successful pictures, but his fame had blossomed spectacularly in the last couple of years in a television series called *For the Defense*, a detective drama in which he played Grant Adams, a defense counsel for wrongly accused, usually attractive women. Not owning a television, Sydney hadn't seen the show more than once or twice.

As she watched him near her, she could see that Garrett was taller than she'd expected. He had one of those elegant male bodies associated with Olympic track stars and swimmers. And though he gave an impression of strength, it seemed more a result of the way he carried himself than due to bulky muscles. His face was largely obscured by his dark glasses, but Sydney knew from pictures she had seen that he had beautiful eyes, great cheekbones and a long narrow nose that gave his face an aristocratic air.

But it was his wide, wry mouth that saved him from being too pretty. In every role she had seen him in there had been a mocking, vaguely naughty irreverence in his smile that said he didn't take things too seriously. That,

as far as Sydney was concerned, saved his looks from
being vapid. And it was his smile that drew her as he
neared the closed gate.

She felt her heart begin to race as he came up to her,
and she wasn't quite sure why, unless it was nerves.
Stars per se didn't knock her on her heels. She'd met
plenty of them over the years, particularly as a young-
ster when her mother took her to the studios as regu-
larly as most kids went to Brownie meetings.

Garrett ran his fingers back through his dark auburn hair, glistening with deep mahogany highlights in
the sun. His mouth grew wider. Though there was an
air of friendliness about him, Sydney didn't think of
him that way. Almost by definition, the man was a
threat, a danger—the personification of everything
about Hollywood that she deplored.

"Got a pencil?" he asked before Sydney could speak.

"A pencil?" She was caught off guard by the question.

"Yeah, something to write with." He patted the
pocketless front of his silk shirt. "I don't have anything."

Sydney swung her purse off her shoulder and dug
around until she found a ballpoint pen. She handed it
over. Garrett's mouth twisted with amusement.

"I'll need something to write on," he said, his hand
poking toward her through the bars.

"Do I look like a secretary?" she snapped before she'd
managed to squelch the comment. She sucked in her
breath and watched him carefully, but there was no way
to discern his reaction to her comment. His eyes were
completely obscured by the tinted lenses of his glasses.
She pulled an old grocery list from her purse and
handed it to him, waiting to see what was next.

He turned the paper over and began writing. Then, as he looked up, his smile broadened—from the way his head moved, Sydney could tell he was scanning her body. He handed everything back through the bars, his teeth gleaming. "Are you visiting, or are you from L.A.?" he asked.

She blinked. "Pardon?"

"Just curious. You don't look like . . . most of them."

Garrett gestured toward the slip of paper, which she read. It simply said, "To a gorgeous girl. Best wishes, Zinn Garrett." Sydney shook her head with confusion. "What's this?"

"My autograph. What did you expect me to write, 'Tom Selleck'?"

Suddenly she realized what had happened and laughed. "I'm afraid you've misunderstood, Mr. Garrett. I'm not here for an autograph."

He pushed his glasses up into his hair, exposing his eyes. They had an ironic twinkle—and not the remotest trace of embarrassment. "You mean you're not an autograph hound?"

She shook her head.

"What, may I ask, do you want, then? No, let me guess," he said, lifting his hand. "You're a process server. My ex and her lawyer are at it again." He surveyed her body again. "The short skirt, the legs, the enticing mouth are to lure me into range."

The consummate actor, he'd delivered the speech flawlessly. He was as supple as a cat, able to land on all fours, no matter what.

She shook her head again, then took off her sunglasses. "If that were my purpose, you'd already have the summons in your hand."

Garrett rubbed his chin. "Good point."

He looked into her eyes, and she looked into his. Zinn Garrett's were indeed beautiful—green-hazel. Stars, all stars, were interesting to see in the flesh. In photographs and on film their familiar faces were hopelessly trapped in a two-dimensional medium. In person they always seemed more real, more fallible. Sydney remembered that about her father when she'd seen him once when she was twelve.

He continued to assess her. "You're not a robber or a hit lady. I'd already be dead."

She smiled, reluctant to end the game. "True."

He put his hands on his hips. "If I had an easel with me I suppose we could play Win, Lose or Draw. But seeing as I don't, how about a hint?"

"All right."

Sydney reached into her purse and removed her nickel-plated 9-mm Heckler & Koch semiautomatic. She had the grace not to point it at him, but he blanched anyway.

"I'm Sydney Charles, Mr. Garrett," she said. "And if you'd already hired me to provide security for your family, I wouldn't have allowed you to walk out here to talk to a perfect stranger at the gate."

Garrett swallowed hard, but he didn't flinch. "You're Sydney Charles?"

"Yes, and we had an appointment—" she checked her watch "—thirty-five minutes ago."

He managed to pull himself together and regain his aplomb. "I apologize for being late, Miss Charles, and I hope you'll forgive me for thinking you were a fan. I didn't realize who you were because, frankly, I was expecting a man."

"It happens often," she replied, still enjoying her advantage. "The astute observer will notice, however, that my name is spelled with a *Y*, not an *I*."

"Maybe," Garrett admitted wryly, "I need to brush up on my spelling, as well as my security practices."

Sydney nodded. "I agree. You do."

Her directness seemed to amuse him. "Well," he said, pointing at the gun, "if you'll put that thing away, maybe we can have our meeting."

She slid the pistol back into her purse, glancing at him with more than a little self-satisfaction. Garrett seemed to notice, but refrained from comment. The autographed scrap of paper was still in her hand so, unable to resist the urge, she poked it through the bars at him. "Seeing that I can't use this, maybe you can send it along to the Smithsonian."

He took the paper. Then, seeing the expression on his face, Sydney immediately realized she had gone too far. It was hardly the hand-kissing that Abe Cohen had referred to in their conversation. To Garrett's credit, though, he seemed to take the barb in stride.

After crumpling the paper and stuffing it into his pocket, he said, "One thing I've learned, playing the role of Grant Adams. Never argue with a woman packing a gun."

He dropped his sunglasses back down on his nose and Sydney put hers on, as well. Garrett went to the security panel where he punched in the code, and the gate swung open. When it had closed, they slowly walked up the driveway together.

"So, you're a private investigator and you're going to protect my daughter?" he asked.

"That's what I had in mind."

"Security's become my preoccupation, I have to tell you. The last thing I want is for something to happen to Andrea because of what I do for a living."

"Recognizing the danger is the first step," she said, taking extra-long strides to keep up with him.

Zinn suddenly stopped and turned to her. There was a slight edge in his voice, to let her know how serious he was. "I might as well be honest with you up front, Miss Charles. I'm very particular about who I hire for this job. It's not going to be automatic, simply because Abe recommended you. Very likely, it'll be someone else."

Sydney felt her stomach drop, but refused to give up. She tried to sound self-confident. "I know you haven't offered me the job, but then, I haven't exactly agreed to take it, either, have I?"

"You've got your lines down pretty well," he remarked, a sly grin playing at the edge of his mouth. "How do you prepare for these interviews? Read a little Ellery Queen?"

Sydney felt herself turn red. Perhaps she'd come across more cheeky than self-assured. "Mr. Garrett, I only meant to say I've got to feel good about a job or there's no point in taking it. A good fit is in everybody's interest."

She saw the skepticism on his face, but he didn't comment, much to her relief. As they continued walking, she reminded herself that she needed this guy. Badly. A week working for Zinn Garrett would probably pay the rent on an apartment for two or three months—not to mention the fact that his name would do wonders for her résumé. She couldn't afford to let the opportunity get away.

"If I sounded snide, I apologize," she said, when he didn't respond to her last comment. "In my line of work, a person tends to get a little hard-bitten."

He gave a slight laugh. "You don't look hard-bitten to me. In fact, if you want to know the truth, I'd say you were miscast. Except when you pulled that pistol out of your purse, you haven't struck me as intimidating at all." He gave her thick braid a playful tug. "Sam Spade, you're not."

Sydney fumed silently. His familiarity and his patronizing tone annoyed her. But it was important that she find a way to make him take her seriously. "Appearances can be deceiving," she said, restraining herself.

"That's an argument I can relate to," he replied. "I think all actors have that problem to some degree—the image thing. Like the way people are always confusing me with my character on the show."

"You won't have that problem with me," she told him sweetly. "I don't watch television."

Garrett chuckled. "My sponsors would definitely be unhappy to hear that."

"Nothing personal," she said quickly, realizing she might have offended him once more.

"Hey, don't worry. Not everybody loves Grant Adams. Hell, sometimes I get a little sick of him myself."

"Do you?"

There must have been incredulity in her voice, because he stopped and looked at her. They were at the foot of the steps leading up to the front door. "I know you assume I'm some kind of Hollywood bimbo, Miss Charles. And frankly, I don't care what you think about me personally. But if you're serious about this job, there's one thing you might as well know up front. I take security for Andrea to be a deadly serious matter. At the moment it's the number-one priority in my life."

Sydney looked directly at him. "I understand. And I'm glad to hear it."

"And, to be fair, you might as well know I really have got somebody else in mind for the job. I'm talking to you because, in effect, Abe asked me to. But I don't want you to get your hopes up."

Sydney took off her glasses again so that he could see the sincerity in her eyes. "It doesn't matter who I'm up against," she said. "I'm confident I can do the job. I know my ability."

Garrett's mouth twisted with amusement, like a man who knew he was in the catbird seat. "You've been saying all the right things, Sam, so I'll give you honest consideration. But I won't promise more."

"All I ask is that you have an open mind."

Zinn Garrett pushed his glasses back up into his hair again, apparently wanting to show some sincerity of his own. His eyes were moving back and forth between hers, the way they surely did every time his role called for him to be seductive. Then he rested his arm on her shoulder, as a person would talking to their very best friend. "What do your friends call you, Miss Charles?"

She was so taken aback by the sudden cordiality that she could only sputter, "Syd, mostly."

"Mind if I call you that?"

She shook her head.

"Listen, Syd, I don't know what Abe said to you, but I want one thing clear. When my kid is at issue, all the Hollywood crap goes out the window. I don't care if you're purple and have two heads, if you're the best one for the job, you get it. By the same token, a plunging neckline and dynamite legs don't count for much. Believe it or not, I'm capable of keeping my pants zipped. I don't how all this sounds to you, but I don't want there to be any misunderstandings." His green-hazel gaze skittered to her lower lip, seemingly to belie his words.

It took a moment, but Sydney regained her composure. "Frankly, Mr. Garrett, I couldn't be more pleased." Smiling sweetly, she then took his arm and gently removed it from her shoulder. "And in case you're wondering, I can keep my pants zipped, too."

Zinn Garrett's wide mouth spread into a self-satisfied grin. "Syd, I think it's time to go inside and meet Andrea."

2

HE OPENED THE DOOR. Sydney stepped inside and was nearly bowled over by a little girl coming toward them at full speed through the entry hall. The child, about four, was practically naked. She had on the bottom of a swimsuit, but not the top.

"Daddy, Da—" Her shriek died mid-word as she skidded to a halt a few feet from Sydney. Her expression was startled, but she immediately wedged past the unexpected visitor to her father.

Zinn swept the child into his arms.

"¡Dios mio!" The voice was coming from the inner sanctum of the house.

Sydney looked back to see a short, corpulent Mexican woman coming at a half run, her heels clicking on the tile floor. The top of the child's swimsuit was dangling from her hand.

"¡Dios mio!" she repeated, distraught. "I am so sorry, Señor Garrett. She was out of my arms in a flash."

Zinn was hugging the child, rocking her back and forth, their cheeks pressed together. "That's all right, Yolanda. You knew it was Daddy, didn't you, angel?"

The woman looked at Sydney, her face filling with embarrassment. She shrugged helplessly.

"Yolanda," he said, "this is Sydney Charles, the security specialist I told you about."

The housekeeper looked confused. "But señor, you say it was a man coming, not a beautiful young lady."

Zinn laughed. "I was surprised at first, too. But believe me, she's tough as nails." He gave Sydney a wink, which she pointedly ignored. "This is my housekeeper, Yolanda," he said, continuing the introductions. "Of late she's been doubling as Andrea's bodyguard." He stroked Andrea's head. "And I don't have to tell you who this monkey is."

The little girl, who had hair much the same color as her father's, turned suddenly shy, resting her head on his shoulder.

Sydney touched her cheek. "Hi, Andrea," she said brightly. "It looks to me like you're getting ready for a swim."

She nodded, then turned her face away to hug her father.

"She has been hungry to swim for an hour, *señorita*," Yolanda moaned. "She thinks she is French—" the woman dangled the top of the child's swimsuit from her finger "—and doesn't like this one."

"It's my fault," Zinn explained. "I promised she could go swimming as soon as I got home." He turned to Sydney. "I don't like her in the pool unless I'm here." He closed the front door and put Andrea down. "You go with Yolanda and finish getting ready, okay, angel face?" he said to the child. "Daddy will meet you out by the pool in a few minutes." He watched Andrea run off down the hallway.

She could see that Abe Cohen had been right about Zinn's devotion to his daughter, but somehow she hadn't expected it to be as sincere as it appeared. In fact, the man was constantly surprising her and catching her off guard.

People in the entertainment business usually weren't renowned for their wonderful marriages or happy family lives. Sydney had heard the details about Zinn

Garrett's divorce from her mother, who kept up with Hollywood gossip.

Apparently Monica Parrish had married Garrett just as his career was taking off. An aspiring actress herself, she hadn't been able to accept the strain of him making it big when her own career was stalemated.

After Andrea was born, the marriage went from bad to worse. The couple fought over values and priorities, and Monica ended up suing for divorce. But by then, her own career was beginning to take shape, so Zinn became the primary parent. That gave Andrea stability, while affording Monica the chance to concentrate on her acting.

"Well," he asked, turning his attention back to Sydney, "what do you think of my progeny?"

She couldn't help smiling. He seemed so typically the proud father. "She's a lovely child."

Zinn observed her for a moment, noting her bemused expression. He decided that she was really a most attractive woman—and in more ways than just a physical sense. Her demeanor was appealingly different from the women he normally encountered.

Most of the actresses he worked with tended to be somewhat self-possessed. Status, pecking order and star power were, after all, the name of the game in Hollywood. And the women he met who weren't in the film business usually seemed incapable of seeing through the celluloid veneer masking him. But Sydney Charles struck him as almost disdainful of his status, and in a rather intriguing way.

She appeared neither to be intimidated by him, nor to like him particularly, which, if nothing else, was a refreshing change. Of course, had she not been so appealing, he might not have found the situation so compelling.

Zinn nodded toward her purse. "I don't suppose you pack a bikini along with a pistol in that thing, do you?" he questioned.

She looked perplexed. "No. Why do you ask?"

"You seem so well prepared, I thought you might have one around for whatever occasion arises. To be more precise, I thought you might wish to come swimming with Andrea and me."

The prospect didn't seem to please her, because her expression turned frosty. "I don't make a habit of interviewing in a swimsuit," she replied.

His gaze drifted down to her cleavage and back up again. Her blue eyes were waiting for him—darts and daggers under a veil of cool restraint. "I see," he said.

"You *are* interested in security for your daughter, aren't you, Mr. Garrett?" Her voice was coolly professional.

"Yes, indeed."

"Then perhaps we should get on with the interview, and forget about socializing."

"I wasn't thinking in terms of 'socializing,' as you put it. The fact of the matter is I don't want to keep Andrea waiting for her swim, and at the same time I realize I've already kept you cooling your heels for much too long. I thought maybe we could kill two birds with one stone—talk a bit and have a swim."

"Oh." She seemed momentarily embarrassed. "I misunderstood."

The apology on her face was somewhat qualified. Zinn didn't mind, though. He found the situation rather amusing. The truth was, he wouldn't have minded seeing her in a bikini, even if that hadn't been his primary consideration. "I also thought that since swimming is Andrea's favorite activity these days, it wouldn't hurt to find out how you handled yourself in the water."

She listened, but didn't appear convinced.

"You do swim?" he asked, pressing his newfound advantage.

"Oh, yes. Quite well. As a teenager I was a certified lifeguard."

"First aid, CPR, that sort of thing?"

"Yes. I felt it was important, considering the nature of my work." She watched him watching her. Then she said, "I suppose I could demonstrate my skills sometime, if you really consider it important."

"No. I'll take your word for it." Zinn allowed a smile to creep across his face. He found he liked jousting with her. "Well, perhaps we'd better get on with our discussion, then."

He took her by the arm and they started walking back through the long entry hall. "We're not very formal here. Please do me a favor. Call me Zinn."

"All right. Whatever you wish."

At the end of the hall an arched doorway led to a sunroom filled with wicker chairs with fluffy cushions and pillows, lots of plants and primitive sculpture. They went on through to a large brick patio where Zinn gestured for her to sit at a table under a turquoise umbrella. He took the chair opposite her as she gazed across the expanse of lawn toward the pool. The view over West Los Angeles was magnificent. The whole house—what she'd seen of it—was fabulous. Decorator perfect.

Sydney turned her attention back to Zinn, folding her hands in front of her on the table. She was no longer sure what to expect from the man, but she decided to start the interview on her own terms, rather than wait for him. "What can I tell you about myself?"

"Well, I do have some questions."

She waited.

"Do you have a business card with you?"

"Yes."

"Could I see it?" he asked.

Sydney fished one out of her purse and handed it to him. Zinn studied it. "Funny thing. I called this number after I spoke with Abe. The phone's been disconnected."

She saw what he was getting at and colored. "I moved recently. The telephone company hasn't gotten the new-number message connected yet."

"I see." He continued studying the card. "This address. I drove by the place on my way home. It's an apartment complex in Santa Monica. Modest, but nice enough, I suppose." His eyes engaged hers. "Did you really have your office there?"

"My office is in Glendale now."

"In an office building?" he pressed.

"Look, I don't need a fancy office suite to be competent."

He looked directly into her eyes. "It's in your home, in other words."

"Yes. Well . . . to be perfectly honest, it's in my mother's home. But it's only temporary. I'm looking for new quarters."

Garrett handed her back the card. He had the grace to look a little embarrassed for her. Sydney felt her cheeks start to burn.

"Can I ask you a blunt question?" he continued. "How many cases of this nature has your agency handled?"

Sydney remembered Abe's advice about acting as though she were on top of the world. But how could she lie? She'd never been dishonest. Sighing, she answered, "None . . . exactly like this one."

"How many, period?"

"A few small things. I've only been on my own for two months. But I'm not inexperienced, Mr. Garrett. I was with Candy Gonzalez at Los Angeles Security and Investigations for almost a year. We protected Gwen Adams when that estranged fiancé of hers and his wacko girlfriend were on the loose, making threats."

"Did you handle the security *personally?*"

"Well, Candy certainly didn't go to the ladies' room with her!"

Zinn smiled mildly.

"On a case in Anaheim," Sydney went on, "I tracked down a four-year-old boy whose father had kidnapped him from the mother. Then I provided security for the boy until the guy was arrested. What I did was similar enough to the requirements here to demonstrate my competence."

"That makes me feel somewhat better. Not that it's likely to make much difference," he added casually. "My principal consideration has to be Andrea."

"And if you hire me, it will be mine, too." Sydney's blood was pulsing, and it wasn't only because the battle was at last joined; Zinn Garrett was keeping her off balance with his feinting and bobbing. One minute it looked as if he was half ready to proposition her; the next he seemed intent on making her out the fool. "Let me ask you a direct question, Mr. Garrett. Do you really care whether I have any relevant experience or not?"

He blinked. "Meaning?"

"Meaning I want to know if this is a serious interview, or if you're just having fun with me."

He hesitated for a moment before answering. "Earlier, I would have said that I was going through the motions because Abe asked me to. What I told you then is true— I've virtually decided to hire someone else. But there's something about you that fascinates me. You're a little different. I like that."

Sydney took a deep breath, wondering just how blunt she could afford to be. "I'm not auditioning for a role on your show."

"True. But I'm not hiring a bookkeeper, either. There's a personal dimension involved here."

There was a plaintive cry from inside the house. They both glanced toward the sun-room. Zinn Garrett's daughter seemed as impatient with the pace of things as Sydney, who felt totally frustrated. "If the job's still available, I'd like a chance to make my case. Just hear me out. Please."

Zinn reached over and took her hand in a benevolent sort of way. Sydney felt her body turn into a block of granite at his touch. Her breathing stopped involuntarily.

"All right," he said, "if you want to make a pitch, I'll listen. But would you mind if I have a brief swim with Andrea first? It'll only take a few minutes." He got up without waiting for a reply. "I'll just slip on a suit and be right back out."

He went to the door of the sun-room, then stopped and turned back to her. "I don't mean to sound negative, Sydney, but I've also got Andrea's mother to think about. My ex-wife doesn't exactly put our daughter at the center of her universe, but she is aware of what's happening, and she's concerned. For the moment she's out of my hair—in Africa on location. But if Monica comes back before this thing is taken care of, she'll start second-guessing me. So you see my predicament."

With his hand on the doorframe, he perused her as though he was taking inventory. "I'll do my best to keep an open mind, but no promises on the outcome, okay?" He punctuated the comment with a smile. "Yolanda will be out shortly. Let her know what you'd like to drink. Oh, and one other thing. While you're waiting, just relax. My bark is much worse than my bite." He gave her that wry smile of his, and went inside.

Sydney stared at the empty doorway. The guy couldn't have performed more smoothly if he'd had a script to work from. She shook her head, not really sure what had happened, or if she should feel humiliated, hopeful or irate.

One thing that really annoyed her was the certainty with which he plied his appeal. He was really hard to ignore. That taunting mouth of his almost dared her to put him down, and yet he absorbed her blows with such innocent self-deprecation, dancing around her like a clever prizefighter feinting with his prey.

There was no question of his not taking her seriously, although it wasn't entirely clear what he was doing. The business about the bikini was completely unprofessional, but he'd managed to wriggle out of it. Slippery, that's what he was. Sydney just hoped she didn't appear to be falling for his game, because that was the last thing she wanted. What confused her was why he couldn't see that.

Of course, the important thing was that she was still in the match. The first round might have gone to him, but she wasn't out of it. She'd give him her best shots, but she knew she had to be careful. The key, she decided, was to keep things on track. She had to make *him* listen to *her*.

Wanting to stretch her legs, Sydney got up and wandered over to the pool. It was really huge—not all that much smaller than the pool at her former high school in Glendale. For a few minutes she stared into the crystalline water, thinking. Absently she tickled her cheek with the tip of her braid, pondering the arguments she would make. The key had to be in the case itself—the nature of the threat to Andrea.

From what Sydney had read in the paper, some mystery woman had been harassing Zinn for a long time—apparently obsessed with him. But it wasn't until she'd begun threatening Andrea's safety that things had turned scary.

Recently she had made an attempt to kidnap the little girl when she'd gone to the supermarket with the housekeeper. That had been the last straw for Zinn. He'd decided full-time protection for his daughter was required.

Sydney had no doubt about the sincerity of Zinn's concern. But she saw her best chance at the job was to convince him that he needed more than just protection for Andrea; he had to find out who the crazy woman was and eliminate her threat. That would take Sydney more into the area of crime detection, but she was fairly sure that the best defense was a good offense—particularly since the adversary was yet unknown.

The question was whether she'd be able to convince Zinn of her strategy. With a sigh she returned and installed herself at the umbrella table alongside the pool. She folded her arms and gazed off into the hazy vista, wondering if she was fooling herself, or if she really did have a shot at the job.

She'd been sitting there a few minutes when she heard giggling coming from inside the house. Andrea Garrett was at the sliding-glass door to the sun-room. The housekeeper was standing behind her. Yolanda gave the girl a little nudge. Seeming to find her courage, the child started out into the yard. As she neared, Sydney knew instinctively what Andrea was feeling—after all, meeting strange adults could be every bit as trying for a four-year-old as a job interview was for her.

"What you want to drink, *señorita?*" Yolanda called from the shade of the house as the girl made her way around the pool. "You want beer?"

Sydney shook her head. "No, I'd prefer juice or iced tea. Whatever you have."

"You watch the *niña*, no?"

"Sure, I'll watch her."

Yolanda nodded and went inside. Andrea came up to Sydney. The little girl studied her, unconsciously curling her toes in the rubber thongs she wore.

"You look nice, Andrea, in your pretty pink swimsuit."

There was no response.

"Do you like to swim?"

She nodded silently.

"I do, too." Sydney smiled, hoping to soften the apprehensive expression on the child's face. That didn't seem to work, so she reached out and touched Andrea's arm, running her fingers lightly along her soft skin.

Sydney had always loved children, though she hadn't been around them much. When she was, there was a natural affinity. Some people attracted cats, some attracted children. Sydney seemed to attract both.

Andrea then shyly slipped her hand into Sydney's, seeming to relish the connection between them. There was an honesty and innocence in the gesture that was touching.

"Do you like my daddy?" Andrea abruptly asked.

Sydney laughed. "Why, yes, he's a very nice man."

"Lots of ladies like him."

"I'm sure they do." Sydney stroked the child's head, and pulled her closer, gently tickling her ear.

"Every lady in the whole world does."

"Well, that might be a bit of an exaggeration, but he's pretty popular, I admit." She brushed back Andrea's hair. "What gave you that idea, anyway?"

"Yolanda says so."

"Well, then, maybe it's true."

Andrea inched a bit closer. She seemed to like the affection. "Can I sit on your lap?"

Sydney was surprised at how quickly Andrea had warmed up to her. "Sure."

In just a moment Andrea was perched on her lap, looking quite content. "Yolanda says you're pretty," she said.

"That's very nice of her."

"I think you are, too."

"Thank you, Andrea. I think you're pretty, also. And you have the nicest cheeks," she said, giving one of them a pinch.

Andrea giggled and tilted her head shyly. Then she studied Sydney with a serious face. "Daddy loves me."

"Of course, he does. You're his little girl."

"Do you have a little girl?"

"No. But if I did, I'd want her to be as nice as you."

Andrea smiled, and again lapsed into silence. Then she reached out and took the long blond braid hanging down the front of Sydney's shoulder, fondling it curiously between her fingers.

"How come you only got one?"

"It's only half the work of two," she replied wryly.

Andrea failed to see the humor. "Yolanda makes two for me."

"I bet they're very pretty ones, too."

The girl nodded immodestly. "My mommy isn't married to my daddy anymore."

"Does that make you sad?"

Andrea shook her head slowly. Sydney sensed the response was less than totally honest, and she felt a pang of sadness for her. But there was no particular emotion on the child's face. "Mommy doesn't love Daddy anymore," she said matter-of-factly.

"That's rough, isn't it, sweetheart?" Sydney replied, running the backs of her fingers over Andrea's cheek. "But one lucky thing—you get to see both your mommy and your daddy. When I was little, I never got to see my daddy."

"How come?"

"I don't think he wanted to have a little girl, so he pretended he didn't."

"That's mean."

"That's what I thought, too. But now I'm big, so I don't worry about it anymore. Just think how nice it is that you have a daddy who loves you."

Andrea smiled at the happy thought.

"Well, well," a voice came from across the pool. "I see one Garrett is succeeding with you."

Hearing her father, Andrea jumped off Sydney's lap and hurried around the pool to meet him. Zinn swept her up into his arms.

He was in brief swim trunks—shiny black ones that seemed made for his muscular physique. His thighs and shoulders were nicely shaped and well-toned.

He was a marvelous specimen, and Sydney found her eyes glued to him as he moved around the pool with lithe, graceful strides, carrying his daughter in one arm.

There wasn't an ounce of self-consciousness or embarrassment in the man—doubtless because of all the hours he'd spent under the critical eye of the camera. She recalled her own father's aloof, self-assured manner—a confidence that was terribly appealing, despite everything.

It wasn't until he was standing before her, his feet casually apart, his chest a billboard of masculine sexuality, that she recalled her earlier displeasure with him. That mocking smile of his revived her former pique.

"Glad the two of you are getting acquainted," he said.

Andrea was running her hand over Zinn's furry chest, caressing it as she might her teddy bear. Sydney understood the impulse. It was one of the more attractive chests she'd ever seen. She pulled her gaze away from him and responded, "We've got a lot in common."

"You either like children, or find it convenient. Mind if I ask which?" Zinn said, observing her.

"I do like kids, even though it happens to be politic to say so."

"I believe you," he replied, lapsing back into his easy charm. He put his daughter down and pointed to the shallow end. "Go splash some water on your face and tummy, angel face. I'll be there in a minute."

Andrea slipped out of her thongs and dashed gleefully toward the far end of the pool. Zinn watched her go, a big grin on his handsome face, then he turned back to Sydney. "I often wonder how my ex and I ever produced her. Between Monica's acid tongue and my ego, the kid has a lot of genes to overcome," he said with a laugh. He watched Andrea cupping water from the pool and splashing it over herself. "You know Abe very well?" he asked, without taking his eyes off his daughter.

"Not really. I know him through my mother. And she knew him back in the days when he represented my father."

"Your father?"

She took a deep breath, glad to get it over with. "Yes. Dick Charles."

Zinn whipped his head toward her. "Dick Charles was your old man?"

"Yes."

He contemplated her. "I don't recall Dick having—"

"He did, though on the wrong side of the blanket, as they say."

He slowly nodded. "I believe I did hear that story, come to think about it."

"Well," she said blandly, "you're looking at the living proof."

Zinn looked thoughtful. "Wasn't a very happy circumstance, I take it."

"It was a long time ago, Mr. Garrett. I don't think about it anymore."

"How is it you never got into the business?"

She concentrated on keeping her tone light, though she hated answering these kinds of questions. "Because I didn't want to."

"You've got the equipment," he said, surveying her casually.

"My equipment, as you put it, is hardly the reason I'm here," she snapped, finally losing control.

Zinn Garrett smiled. "I seem to be straying into troubled waters a little more with you than I usually do with people. You have my apologies."

"Daddy, *come on!*" Andrea implored.

Garrett pulled the towel from his neck and swept his glasses off in one smooth motion, handing them to Sydney. Startled, she took them. He peered down at her, and before he turned away he said, "Actually, I kind of like it that you're different. Shows you're not just another pretty face with a million-dollar body, huh?"

Sydney didn't even manage a gasp before he sauntered off to his daughter. Despite telling herself that she needed this job, her first reaction was to get up and walk out. But he had her trapped. She wondered if he had sensed how desperate she was, or if he always acted this way. Upon reflection, she decided it was probably just part and parcel of his giant ego. He was a star, and that meant he was used to getting his own way.

Meanwhile Zinn had gone to the far end of the pool where he bent over, coiling his body, before skimming out over the water, executing a perfect racing dive. He did a rapid length of the pool and back, then stopped where Andrea stood waiting. At his urging, the little girl did her best imitation of his feat and the two of them swam together, Zinn taking her hand now and then to afford her some rest. When she'd finally made it to the deep end, he turned proudly toward Sydney.

"How about that?"

"Bravo, Andrea. Well-done," she replied, pointedly looking only at the child.

They swam back to the side of the pool, in front of Sydney, where they stopped. Andrea's face appeared over the edge. Her smile was not unlike her father's. Before they pushed off again, Zinn gave Sydney some sort of meaningful look. The trouble was, she wasn't quite sure what it meant.

Games in the pool continued as Yolanda arrived with a tray of drinks and snacks. She put everything on the table, placing the iced tea in front of Sydney before withdrawing.

Sydney sipped her drink for the next ten minutes, watching father and daughter at play. Her feelings oscillated between irritation at the way she'd been treated, and admiration for his loving manner toward Andrea.

The interview wasn't going at all the way she'd planned. She'd had him pegged right, though. He was a typical actor—full of charm and guile, and with an ego the size of a national park. Unfortunately, she'd assumed that being aware of that would be all the insulation she needed. In retrospect, she wondered if maybe she'd been overly confident.

Soon the play in the pool ceased and Zinn and his daughter climbed out. Andrea made a beeline for the chips and juice. Zinn slowly ambled over and picked up his towel. Standing before her, he dried himself, then dropped down into the chair next to her. He poured the bottle of beer Yolanda had brought into a chilled mug and took a long drink.

"Sydney," he said, "there's something about your expression that tells me you're not pleased with me."

She handed him back his sunglasses. "Is it that obvious?"

"I get the unmistakable impression you don't approve of me at all—which is okay, of course. Everybody's entitled to his or her opinions. But I'm curious why."

"It's nothing personal."

"Then it's true."

She gave him her most professional smile. "Well, I'm not into . . . Hollywood games. Let's put it that way."

He sipped his beer. "Would you believe me if I said I wasn't, either?"

Her smile faded. "Not particularly."

"You're direct, Syd. I'll give you that."

"Is this relevant?" she asked.

"I always look at the whole person."

She wasn't sure, but she had a feeling that under the sunglasses, he was examining her cleavage again. "Apparently you're a psychologist, as well as an actor."

"Actors, if they're good, are students of human nature. To become someone else you have to understand motivation. To stay in character means to live in another person's skin." Andrea, who'd been munching on chips, offered her father some from the bowl. "No, thank you, honey."

"So," Sydney continued, "I'm talking to Grant Adams now. Is that what you mean?"

"Absolutely not. The only place I act is in front of the camera. And I do it then because I'm well paid. My personal life is another matter entirely."

Sydney wasn't going to argue with him. She was skeptical, but it didn't really matter. Even apparent sincerity could be ingenuine.

They were both silent for a minute, then Sydney spoke. "You know, it seems to me that the only thing that really matters is whether or not I can get along with Andrea. That's what is relevant." She looked at the little girl, who was completely oblivious to the adult conversation.

"I've put you off long enough, Syd. You wanted to make a pitch for the job, so go ahead." He took another sip of beer.

Sydney gulped, not having expected her moment in the spotlight to arrive so abruptly. "Maybe this isn't a conversation for mixed company," she said, indicating Andrea with a nod of her head.

"You're right. Let's stroll around the garden, shall we?"

They got up, Zinn taking his mug of beer with him. He patted Andrea's head. "Sydney and I are going to walk around the yard, angel. You finish your juice, okay?"

Andrea nodded and stuffed a handful of chips into her mouth. As they began strolling along the edge of the pool, Zinn took Sydney's arm, resting his hand in the crook of it as though they were close friends.

She noticed how smooth and bronzed his hand was. The thing to do was ignore it, she decided. When they were beyond hearing range, she stopped and faced him. His hand dropped away. It was now or never.

"I assume," she began, "that what you had in mind for this job is hiring a gorilla to protect Andrea—someone big and intimidating."

"It amounts to that, I suppose."

Sydney began walking again, making him follow her this time. "What's this guy like, the one you'd decided to hire before I came along?"

Zinn smiled, admiring her guts. She was hitting the problem head-on, which showed courage. "Jack's got a track record as long as your arm. He's physically intimidating without being a dummy, and I've dealt with him before. I trust him."

"The last point, I can't change," Sydney admitted. "I'll simply have to rely on your ability to see I'm no less trustworthy."

"Okay," he said indulgently. "What about the rest of it?"

"You've made an assumption that being physically intimidating is somehow important. It isn't. The ability to protect is. What I'm saying is that you've got to look at Andrea's well-being in a broader way. Whoever you hire is going to be spending a lot of time with her. Her emotional security is important, too. The question is, Who would be a better companion for your daughter? Me or some bruiser—even if his IQ is in the Mensa range?"

Zinn looked back across the yard toward Andrea, realizing that Sydney's argument had merit. She was focused on his child, and she was serious about what she was doing. Maybe she was as good as she claimed to be. The notion intrigued him. "You've got a point," he replied mildly.

"The real question is whether Andrea will be safe."

"Granted."

"Assume for a minute I know how to use the HKP 7 I carry in my purse, and that I'm as good in martial arts as my rating attests...."

"Okay...."

"Assume, in other words, defending Andrea's person isn't the issue."

"What *is* the issue, if it's not that?"

Sydney took a deep breath before she spoke. "Eliminating the threat. In other words, getting this woman off the street."

"That's the job of the police," he said, apparently puzzled by the direction of the conversation.

"To the extent they devote the time and resources to it, you're right. But it certainly wouldn't hurt to have a competent investigator at the point of attack. Is this guy, Jack, a P.I., or just a security man?"

"He's a professional bodyguard."

"Well, I'm both. And I'd like to play an offensive role, as well as providing Andrea's security. I'd like to see that this woman, whoever she is, is arrested."

"Her name's Barbara, by the way. I know that much from past experience with her. But the police haven't yet been able to determine her full identity."

"I know from what I've read in the papers that she's been complicating your life, Zinn. What I propose to do is eliminate the problem once and for all."

He was surprised by the proposition. He was even more taken by her enthusiasm and determination. Yet he had trouble separating the detective from the beautiful woman standing before him. Her effect on him was electric, and not all what he would have expected. "You're not what you appear, are you?" he asked, his gaze drifting to her mouth.

Sydney felt a surge of triumph and an unexpected warmth toward the man. With the possibility of victory looming, she almost liked him. And suddenly it didn't matter that the fireworks of sexual attraction were popping at the periphery. That was a sideshow. For the first time, she had the feeling Zinn Garrett was regarding her as a professional. He wasn't discounting her any longer, and that made her feel awfully good.

He took a sip from the mug of beer in his hand. "Tell me, Syd, do you have a specific plan in mind?"

"Until I'd met you and Andrea, and assessed the situation, I couldn't do much planning, but now I have some ideas."

"Share them, if you would."

"Señor Garrett!" It was Yolanda. She was standing at the umbrella table. "Do you wish something more?"

"No," he called to her. "Please take Andrea inside and get her dressed. She's had plenty of snacks."

Andrea wasn't going to go inside so easily, though. She dashed down to where Sydney and Zinn were standing, and leaped into his arms. Zinn gave her a kiss. She said goodbye to Sydney and he put her down again, sending her back to Yolanda with a pat on the bottom. When she'd disappeared into the house, he directed his attention to Sydney.

"You were going to share your ideas."

"Well, obviously, I have to be here to protect Andrea. I think for her sake it's important to downplay the bodyguard angle. I also would want to keep a low profile to lull this Barbara into a false sense of security. I want her overconfident, rather than feeling like she has to get past the security of Fort Knox. With luck, we might even be able to transfer her focus from Andrea to me."

"How would you propose to do that?"

"Well, her behavior isn't easy to anticipate, but if Barbara thinks I'm your new girlfriend, her obsession with you might drive her to target me, instead of Andrea."

He didn't say anything for a moment, as though he was letting the idea sink in. "You're saying that you and I should become lovers and publicize it, to get Barbara to come after you. Then you could grab her."

"In a nutshell."

Zinn smiled, apparently liking the idea. "It would all be for effect, you understand," she said. "I'm not suggesting anything really happen between us. We would simply *pose* as . . . lovers."

"You mean we'd act like lovers. Go through the motions, do the kissy-touchy routine in public, et cetera."

He'd twisted her strategy into a game of sexual innuendo. What did he think? That she'd get into bed with him to add to the realism? "Mr. Garrett, I made the proposal in good faith. I don't want you to think that I in any way intend to have a relationship with you. Actual romance . . . sex . . . is not what I have in mind."

"Perhaps not, but if we're going to be going through the motions, it wouldn't hurt to be friends, would it?"

Sydney shook her head. "For a while, I thought I had your respect as a professional, but now you seem to be acting as though I'm some new starlet on the set you can hit on."

He looked taken aback. "Did I say that? I don't remember making an improper proposal. Our relationship may be professional, but it doesn't have to be antiseptic. I certainly don't fall in love with every actress I work with, but at the same time I appreciate those who are pleasant and avoid garlic and onions before a love scene."

Sydney put her hands on her hips. "I'll tell you what. You give me the job and I won't eat garlic and onions while I'm in your house. How's that?"

Zinn rubbed his chin. "You certainly drive a tough bargain. And I admit I'm impressed with your ideas."

She could hardly contain herself. "You mean I have the job?"

The corners of his eyes crinkled, but he didn't answer her question. Instead he said, "Being a natural skeptic, I'll offer you temporary employment until we see how things work out. Let's call it probation. If you prove satisfactory, we'll make it long-term. Let's say a thousand dollars for three days. That ought to give you a chance to show me what you've got. Will that be agreeable?"

Sydney wasn't absolutely sure whether they were talking about her performance as a security person or otherwise, but the thousand dollars was too tantalizing for her to consider further debate. She chose to interpret the comment as referring to her professional capabilities. She extended her hand toward him. "It's a deal."

Zinn took her fingers like he was accepting a fine piece of china. He drew her hand slowly to his lips. "They never let me do this on the show, Sydney," he said as he peered into her eyes. "And there are so very few occasions in life."

She drew a breath. The shivery sensation she felt each time he touched her reoccurred. Damn his effect on her.

It's just theater, she told herself firmly as his lips brushed her skin. *It doesn't mean a thing—not to him any more than it does to you.* But it was hard to resist Zinn Garrett. And not only because he was attractive. That, she could keep in perspective. There was something about the person emerging from behind the facade that really appealed to her.

When Zinn finally released her hand, he smiled in a way that indicated he was quite pleased with himself. He was really a lot more complicated than she'd first believed. One moment he was one thing; the next, another.

Maybe it would be easier if it was simply raw physical attraction she felt. That was easily understood. Zinn was, after all, one of Hollywood's bronzed gods. And at the moment he was practically naked, standing not two feet from her.

She struggled to remain calm when he reached over and took the braid lying on her breast and fingered it just as Andrea had done earlier. One corner of his mouth twitched slightly at some inner thought. "There's a tiger under this girlish facade of yours, isn't there, Sydney?"

She nodded, staring at his sensuous mouth. She wondered if the charade she'd planned might backfire. How was she ever going to resist him? Had she made a pact with the devil, as her mother had?

Zinn was observing her silently. Sydney felt herself being drawn to him, though she resisted. It seemed for a moment he might even kiss her. Then a wave of panic struck. She turned from him abruptly and started toward the house.

"Hey, Syd, where you going?"

"Home to get my suitcase," she said over her shoulder.

"Your suitcase?"

"Yes, you don't expect me to wear this dress for three days, do you?"

3

LEE LORRAINE WAS ECSTATIC when Sydney told her the news. "Darling, he wants you!"

"For three days, anyway."

She took her daughter by the shoulders and smiled happily into the azure eyes that were the shade of her own. "I couldn't be more pleased for you, Sydney."

They were in the front room of Lee's tidy little bungalow in Glendale. It hadn't changed all that much from when Sydney had grown up there. The photograph of Dick Charles sat in the place of honor on the mantel above the false fireplace. The same furniture, knick-knacks and pictures still decorated the place. Only the leather recliner that Sydney had bought her mother the previous Christmas was new.

"Mom, it's a job, not a marriage proposal."

But Lee didn't pay any attention. She blinked back the moisture in her eyes. "When I heard Zinn Garrett—*the* Zinn Garrett—was looking for someone like you, and that you would actually be living with him," Lee said dreamily, "I regretted everything nasty I'd ever said to you about the gumshoe business."

"Mother, I'm a private investigator. 'Gumshoe' is for old-time movies. And anyway, I won't be living *with* him. I'll be staying in his house to be near his daughter. It's not the same."

Lee smoothed her upswept blond-going-white hair with a graceful hand. Despite her arthritis and other rigors of age, she had managed to maintain much of her once-youthful allure. She was within fifteen pounds of her optimum weight at the peak of her career, and still carried herself with the poise and presence of a performer. She had once been five-six, like Sydney, but had shrunk a bit in recent years.

"Darling," she chided, "don't be so naive. You know perfectly well what he has in mind. He *is* a man, isn't he?"

"Mother!"

"Well, isn't he?"

Sydney glared meaningfully. "That's not the point. It's what *I* have in mind that counts. This is a job. And that's it!"

Lee gave her a stern look and went to the sofa. She patted the cushion next to her, signaling for Sydney to join her. "I'm not suggesting anything unsavory, for heaven's sake," she said when Sydney eased down onto the sofa next to her. "But it's an opportunity, and you should regard it that way."

She gave her mother a sidelong glance. "An opportunity for what?"

Lee sighed the sigh of a mother. "Darling," she replied with what was obviously the most patience she could muster, "the man is a star. You're a gorgeous girl. He knows a million people—people who could help you."

It had always been hard for Sydney to tell what her mother wanted most for her—a husband, or a career in the movies. Sometimes she thought Lee had mixed the two notions into the same glittery dream. But, important as stardom had been to Lee Lorraine, Sydney never doubted that anything had been more vital to her mother's happiness than her love for Dick Charles. If she had to guess, she figured her mother probably wanted for her to be a star married to a star.

"Mom, I'm not an actress. And if I wanted to be discovered, I'd go to a soda fountain. Don't you see that these fairy-tale dreams of yours are out-of-date?"

Lee's lips trembled. It was the same old argument—the one they'd had countless times before. Even so, her mother never passed up an opportunity to give Sydney a nudge toward stardom, her daughter's hostility to the idea notwithstanding. She made sure Sydney saw the tears filling her eyes. "If you knew how many young women would give their eye teeth to—"

"Mother, Zinn Garrett could offer me all of Hollywood and I wouldn't take it. I'm only interested in one thing—protecting his daughter and getting my business on track. If this case didn't involve a little girl, and if I wasn't flat broke, I wouldn't even have taken the job."

Lee pointedly wiped a tear from the corner of her eye. "Will you at least keep an open mind?"

Terrific! They'd slipped into their usual pattern. It had been like that for as long as she could remember. Her mother, an incurable romantic, and Sydney, the pragmatist with her feet planted firmly on the ground.

"Mom, you've let yourself get carried away. The fact that I'm going to be spending a few days with Zinn Garrett doesn't mean I want to change my career plans."

Lee turned away, stifling her response, holding her fingers against her ruby lips. "I'm interfering in your life."

"Don't be silly, Mom. You've saved my tail feathers. If it wasn't for you, I wouldn't have had this opportunity and I'd be out in the street, besides." Sydney touched her mother's cheek. "Please, Mom, accept the fact that I do what I do."

Lee tried to smile at her, blinking back the tears. "Did he think you were pretty?"

Sydney rolled her eyes. "I don't know. We didn't really talk about it." That wasn't strictly true, but she wasn't about to give her mother any false hope.

"Surely you sensed his reaction," Lee coaxed.

Sydney shrugged. "He flirted, I guess. But that's to be expected, isn't it? As you say, he's a man."

"Darling . . ." Always the consummate actress, Lee pretended to struggle valiantly to maintain control. "If you knew how much I want the best for you . . ."

She put her arm around her mother's shoulders. "I know. And I'm grateful, believe me."

That was one thing about Lee Lorraine no one could ever fault—her loyalty and her selflessness. Growing up, Sydney had never doubted her mother's love or dedication. Lee sacrificed and gave of herself at every turn. Now Sydney longed for the opportunity to do something for her mother. That was another reason a paycheck from Zinn Garrett would be welcome.

"I'll be making good money, Mom," she said. "That ought to please you. And if the next few days go well, I could be at this for a while. If so, I'll be back on my feet and out of your hair."

Lee said nothing further. Sydney gave her a kiss, then went to the guest room to pack a case.

The room was the bedroom she'd had as a girl. Lee had kept many of Sydney's high-school mementos, and had put old photographs of her dance recitals back up on the walls. In every direction Sydney turned she could see herself—sometimes toothless, sometimes skinny-legged and flat-chested, but always looking vaguely uncomfortable.

She went over to the photo from her biggest audition at a movie studio. She'd been five at the time, and hadn't been able to keep from breaking into tears when her moment in the spotlight finally came. Needless to say, it had spoiled her chances at stardom, although she was sure she'd gotten as far as she had only because her mother had whispered Dick Charles's name into certain ears.

That painful day—one Sydney was able to relive by simply looking at the picture—had been both the high point and low point of her movie "career." She'd danced until she was eleven to please her mother, but then she'd asserted herself and begun setting her own course in life.

After she'd packed her suitcase, Sydney changed into a pale blue Polo shirt, white cotton pants and espadrilles. Then she took a box of ammunition from the shoe sock in the closet where she'd hidden it, and stuffed it into her purse. Her mother had never seen her gun, and Sydney had no intention of showing it to her. There were certain realities that a mother didn't need to know about. Taking both the purse and suitcase, she headed for the front room.

Lee was at the window and turned when Sydney came into the room. "Darling, what on earth is wrong with your car?"

"What do you mean?"

"There's a big puddle of something under it."

"Oh, no!"

"Is it bad?"

Sydney peered out over her mother's shoulder. "I think my car may just have passed away. The motor was sounding worse and worse on the way over here. Maybe I'd better take a cab to Zinn's. I'll call the garage tomorrow and have them come and pick it up." She opened her purse and pulled out her wallet, finding only a five and a few ones. "I hate to ask, Mom, but do you have forty bucks or so I could borrow until I get paid?"

"Sure, darling. I've got my own Christmas club in the cookie jar. Hang on." Lee hobbled to the kitchen as Sydney silently thanked God for the chance Zinn Garrett had given her.

When her mother returned with the money, Sydney said, "Pay you back in a couple of days, and we're going out to dinner on me."

"Don't be silly. Save your money."

"Mom, dinner is the least you deserve and the least you'll get. Before I'm through, you'll be getting jewels and furs and anything your heart desires."

Lee Lorraine patted her daughter's cheek and said, "If that's the case, darling, you'd better hope Zinn Garrett wants to marry you, not give you a screen test."

Sydney laughed. "I love you, but I don't think quite that much."

Lee instantly looked affronted. "You talk as though it would be a disaster. What I wouldn't have given if your father—" She pressed her lips together and looked apologetic. "Oh, never mind."

Sydney kissed her on the cheek and went to the phone to call a taxi.

THE FORTY DOLLARS BARELY covered the cab fare. Sydney paid the driver, took her suitcase and went to Zinn Garrett's gate. When she'd left, she'd gotten the entry code to the security gate from Yolanda, so she was able to get into the grounds without buzzing up to the house.

Curious about just how adequate the existing security measures were, Sydney took a few minutes to walk along beside the wall in either direction. Despite its height, what she saw had more decorative value than usefulness as protection from intruders. The gate didn't offer much protection, either, if a person willing to incur a few dents in his or her car wished to breach it.

As she trudged up the drive, Sydney tried to decide if it was worth recommending major capital improvements. The walls and fences were adequate to discourage the casual trespasser, but not a determined criminal. To accomplish that, the estate would have to be turned into a virtual fortress. She doubted that would be practical. The key to protecting Andrea would have to be personal surveillance.

Standing at the top of the drive, she scanned the perimeter of the property, making a mental note to check the lights after dark. Proper lighting could do more to deter intruders than all the fences and walls in the world. Wrongdoers almost always sought the darkness. In spite of the fact that the woman she was protecting Andrea from was crazy, Sydney hoped that maxim would apply to her, too.

She was still firmly convinced, though, that her key objective had to be Barbara's arrest. And until she'd spoken with the police detectives conducting the investigation, there wasn't a lot she could do. Even before seeing Abe, Sydney had tried to reach Detective Marvin Kaslow of the L.A.P.D., the officer handling the investigation. Unfortunately, Kaslow had been off for the past two days. But since she knew him, and had worked with him when she was with Candy, she decided to talk to him the next day and get what information she could.

The sun was sinking low in the sky as Sydney climbed the steps to the front door. Before she could ring the bell, the door opened. Yolanda appeared.

"It's you, *señorita*. I wondered when you were coming back. Why you walking around the yard, anyhow?"

"I was studying the security of the grounds."

"The wall, she is very high."

"Yes, it's a good wall."

Yolanda stepped out and took the case from Sydney's hand. "Come. I will show you the room. Dinner is in an hour. Señor Garrett, he say he see you then."

Sydney followed the small heavyset woman through the maze of the house, glancing in at rooms she hadn't seen yet. Though it had been her idea to move in, she couldn't help feeling a little uncomfortable now that she was there. It was one thing to joust with Zinn during a negotiation, but living under the same roof with him could end up being something entirely different.

The guest suite constituted virtually a separate wing of the house. There was a small sitting area with a couple of comfortable chairs in a peach-and-blue floral pattern facing a fireplace. The *chambre* was large and contained a king-size bed, a dressing table, a Chinese armoire and a chaise longue. The draperies, wall coverings and accessories were beautifully coordinated.

Sydney decided the only advantage her apartment in Santa Monica had over it was a kitchen. As she ran her hand lightly over the imported French fabric of the bedspread, she wondered how long it would take before this kind of luxury became habit-forming.

"You like it, *señorita*?"

"It's beautiful."

Yolanda watched her with obvious satisfaction for a moment, then said, "Let me tell you something. Personally, I am glad you have come to the house. I worry about the little one since this woman. She almost kill us! She is crazy, that one."

"She won't be troubling you again, Yolanda. You don't have to worry about that."

"But to tell you the truth, *señorita*, I worry for Señor Garrett as much as for the *niña*. He is very worried and not himself since this happen to the little one."

She instinctively reached out and touched the woman's arm. "That's why I'm here now, Yolanda—to put his mind at ease."

The housekeeper shook her head. "It's hard to believe someone so pretty could scare away the bad one." She smiled devilishly. "Maybe Señor Garrett, he likes you for other reasons than because you are a police. What you think?"

Sydney shook her head. "Let's hope not."

Yolanda shrugged as though she wasn't quite sure.

"How long have you worked for him?" Sydney asked.

"For two and a half years, *señorita*. I come after the divorce from the wife."

The way she pronounced the word *wife* indicated a certain degree of disapproval. It wasn't hard to imagine where the housekeeper's sympathies lay, so Sydney didn't bother to ask. But she was curious about Zinn and decided Yolanda was probably a pretty reliable source of information. "How is Zinn to work for, anyway? Is he a good boss?"

"Señor Garrett, he is a very nice man. He has the *machismo*, you know what I mean? And I don't have to tell you how beautiful he is. Any woman can see this for herself, no?"

Sydney nodded. "The trouble with that type, though, is they are very cavalier toward women, especially if they're a TV star. How can a man be normal when he leads this life?"

"I am not sure all what you are saying, *señorita*. The boss is a very important man, this is true. But to me he is always very good. I think the one you see on the TV and the one in this house, they are not the same man."

Sydney was sure the housekeeper was sincere, but it seemed to her that their perspectives might be very different. In fact, during her short acquaintance with Zinn Garrett, Sydney was struck by how interchangeable his charm and Grant Adams's charm had seemed. "Maybe," she said, not wishing to comment further.

"If you want to know what I think," Yolanda said, "since the wife, she left, I think Señor Garrett he is afraid of the women—not afraid on the outside, like a man and his enemies, but afraid on the inside, like a child and his pain."

Sydney studied Yolanda, surprised by the profundity of her thought. "You mean he really loved Monica? Is that what you're saying?"

"No, the opposite of this. He is afraid what might happen again." Yolanda put her finger beside her temple so as to emphasize her own wisdom. "Now I will go. Maybe you would like to change to be even more beautiful for dinner." With that, she left the room.

After Yolanda had gone, Sydney stood by the bed for a long moment, wondering if she had been given some tremendous insight, or if her already confused state of mind had been mixed up even more. After a while, though, she composed herself and opened her suitcase to put away her clothes.

It had been a long, hot day so she decided to bathe again and change before dinner. Maybe she would put on a different dress, too. And change her hair. Lee had told her the braid was nice for picnics, tennis or the beach, but that she ought to show off her beautiful hair more often. "How many girls are blessed with such a lovely head of hair?" she'd said once, not long ago. Sydney decided that a little variety wouldn't be bad. Tonight was as good a time as any.

But first, she climbed into the giant whirlpool bath for a leisurely soak. Her apartment had only a shower, and the tub at her mother's was tiny, so it had been aeons since she'd had a proper bath. *What luxury!*

Later, as she dried herself, she glimpsed her body in the mirrored closet door. She thought about Yolanda's remarks about Zinn. Who was the guy, really? Someone different than who she thought he was? And could what Yolanda have said be true? That underneath he'd been hurt and was gun-shy about women? It certainly wouldn't be the first time that had happened.

Even more confounding was why she seemed to care. Sydney had never been head over heels in love, even as a teenager. Her mother's romantic obsessions had been more than enough for one household. Wanting to avoid her mother's mistakes, she'd always kept somewhat aloof when it came to boys. Not that she had a philosophical aversion to men; she'd had a pretty normal life in college, with dates and boyfriends. But since her graduation she hadn't been out much—at least not to the places where "the action" was, as a friend of hers called it. Criminal investigation didn't actually lend itself to meeting eligible men, and so her romantic life had been pretty nonexistent for over a year.

There had been one exception. A couple of months after Sydney had gone to work for Candy Gonzalez, she'd been assigned to an investigation for a young lawyer named Brent Haydon. He soon showed more interest in her than in the case, and she had gone out with him. They had dated for a couple of months after the investigation was complete, but like so many of the young bachelors around, Brent defined relationships by seasons—ski season, football season, the rainy season, blonde season, brunette season.

If a Yuppie L.A. bachelor didn't change girlfriends with the new season's wardrobe, something was wrong. Sydney had no particular expectations, but she didn't like falling somewhere between a BMW convertible and a state-of-the-art sound system on a guy's scale of values. Intimacy ought to count for more than a hot new Springsteen CD, or a fax machine.

If men insisted on treating sex like food—something you needed whether you noticed the flavor or not— then Sydney wouldn't bother to play the game. Besides, the challenges of starting a new business had sapped her energy. Keeping the wolf from the door had a way of making the petunias in the window box seem unimportant. Now, if she could put this curious fascination she was starting to feel for Zinn Garrett into perspective, she might actually be able to enjoy her turn of luck.

After she slipped on her underwear, she brushed out her hair. She decided to twist it on top of her head. Studying herself in the mirror as she fussed with her hair, she realized it had been a long time since she'd bothered to really fix herself up.

From her limited wardrobe she chose a yellow cotton sundress that had a very low-cut back. It was a bit sexier than she would have liked, but it had survived the suitcase better than any of her other dresses.

By the time she was ready, Sydney felt more like she was going on a date than having dinner at home with the family. Were her feelings toward Zinn Garrett leading her to that conclusion? Or was she already falling into the role he had laid out for her? Acting was as phony as a Hollywood back-lot set. Her mother had bought the dream, and it hadn't made her happy. Sydney was determined to focus squarely on reality.

She wandered out of her room, making two wrong turns before she found the den, a room with fat leather sofas, stone tables and ebony sculptures that looked like they came from Africa. The predominant colors were cream and apricot. Zinn and Andrea were seated side by side, reading a children's storybook. They looked up as she entered the room.

There was delight on Zinn's face as he stared at her. Neither he nor Andrea said anything for a moment.

"Good evening," Sydney managed, suddenly uncomfortable under his scrutiny.

"Daddy!" Andrea exclaimed. "Sydney's pretty!"

"My very thought," Zinn said, rising to his feet. He had on a navy blazer with a soft pink cotton shirt. His hair was still wet from the shower and he smelled delicious.

Zinn moved across the room toward her. There was an intensity in his eyes that seemed to indicate appreciation, but after Yolanda's comments, she couldn't be absolutely sure what he was thinking. There was something unnerving about his gaze and the way his expressive mouth always seemed to be signaling a secret thought.

Even as the realization hit her, the corner of his mouth curved slightly and Zinn took her hand, kissing it more suavely than he had that afternoon. Coming from anyone else, the gesture would have seemed forced or affected. But she already associated it with him, and somehow it worked. As her mother always said, good acting never offended.

Zinn released her hand and stood studying her critically. "If I were directing this picture, my dear, I'd send you back to makeup."

Her hand involuntarily went to her cheek. "What did I do wrong?"

"No mistakes, if that's what you mean." He touched her skin with his fingertips. "I'm not sure how fierce an impression you make. Angels, as they say, aren't very intimidating."

Sydney saw his point and smiled serenely. "You don't have to be an eight-hundred-pound gorilla to protect someone. You simply have to know what you're doing."

Andrea had wandered over to where they stood. Sydney smiled down at her and stroked her head, which now sported a single short auburn braid—clearly in imitation of Sydney's.

"We were reading a story, waiting for our drinks until you arrived," Zinn said. "What can I fix you?"

"How about some mineral water?"

His lip twitched. "Mmm. A racy devil, I see. Do you ever kick back?"

"Not while I'm on duty. And, for the next three days, anyway, that's a twenty-four-hour-a-day proposition."

"Sydney, your dedication is commendable," he replied. He went to a mirrored cabinet against one wall, which contained a hidden bar.

As he fixed the three of them something to drink, Zinn watched her in the mirror. Sydney was, if anything, even more attractive than that afternoon. He liked the way she'd twisted her hair up on her head, with long pale strands swirling up off her neck, drawing attention to its graceful arch.

But despite her appeal, he found himself at a bit of a loss as to how to take her. He wasn't used to feeling off balance around a woman, though he doubted she'd noticed the effect she'd had on him.

Zinn liked women, and had always felt comfortable around them. He could "speak their language," as a lady friend of his once put it. Only occasionally would a woman perplex him to the point where every attempt he made to connect fell short. He was beginning to wonder if Sydney Charles wasn't such a case.

Andrea had taken Sydney's hand and was beaming up at her. "See my hair?"

"Yes, I was noticing how pretty it looks," he heard her reply. "Did you do that yourself?"

His daughter giggled. "No, Yolanda did. It's like yours was!"

Sydney tweaked the little girl's nose. "We could almost be twins, couldn't we?"

He noticed her glance over at him. There was something in her look that seemed ambivalent. It wasn't that she found him unappealing, he was quite sure. To the contrary, when they rubbed up against each other, he knew the sparks flew both ways. Still, there was something standing between them. And the fact that he wasn't sure what it was only compounded its effect.

By the time he had finished preparing the drinks, Andrea had taken Sydney by the hand and led her to the couch. He joined them, serving the drinks. His daughter was chatting away, so he sat back and listened to the conversation, trying to discern what was going on in Sydney Charles's head.

Andrea was relating the story they'd been reading when Sydney had arrived, dwelling on the details of family life depicted in the story. Then she called over to him. "Daddy, guess what? Sydney didn't have a daddy when she was little because he was mean."

"Oh?" He looked up at Sydney.

"I told her my life story," she explained, almost self-consciously. "That's a succinct summary."

"I see." He continued to watch her as he considered his daughter's comment. Whatever Sydney had told the girl, its poignancy hadn't been lost in translation. He wondered if there was something there that he'd missed.

When he was sure in his own mind that Andrea had been around Sydney long enough to become comfortable with her, he suggested that she go help Yolanda for a while. Perhaps it was selfish, but he wanted a little time alone with Sydney.

As the child disappeared from the room, he turned to her and said, "You seem to have a way with kids."

"It's a mutual thing, I guess. Hard to explain."

As she sipped her drink, he gazed at the curve at the nape of her neck. She showed a hint of discomfort under his scrutiny, which amused him. "Funny thing, mutuality between people—how some connect and others don't."

Sydney nodded but didn't say anything.

"What do you suppose accounts for it?" he asked.

She shrugged. "Experience, chemistry. Who knows?"

Zinn swirled the ice cubes in his glass. Then he suddenly asked, "Are you involved with anyone?"

Sydney blinked. "You mean romantically?"

"Yeah. Is there anybody special in your life?"

"No."

"That's surprising. Somebody as attractive as you are . . ."

"Is there a law that says the two things have to go together?" she asked, a touch of pique in her voice.

He deliberately kept his tone light. "No, it was merely an observation."

She revolved the glass of mineral water in her hands. "Are you seeing someone?" she asked.

"No. Not at the moment."

"Well, then?"

Zinn heard the challenge in her voice. He could see that he'd managed to land square in her brier patch again. "That gives us something in common, doesn't it?"

She took a sip of her water. "Considering our relationship of employer-employee, I don't see the significance."

He contemplated her, looking long and hard into her unyielding blue eyes. "Why is it that Andrea gets on so well with you, whereas I seem to fail so miserably? Is it because she's a female and four?"

Sydney shifted uncomfortably. "I don't hate men, if that's what you're getting at."

"That isn't what I was suggesting."

"Maybe you're too used to women falling all over themselves to get to you, Zinn."

"Ah." He let out a long sigh, suddenly realizing what the problem was. "You've been making assumptions about me."

She shook her head. "I haven't made assumptions. You were the one who brought it up."

He noticed how defensive she sounded. Zinn quaffed his drink and put the glass down on the coffee table. When he sat back, he moved his arm to the back of the sofa. His hand rested behind Sydney's head. He'd been aware of her neck and her bare back since she'd first come into the room. Following an impulse, he brushed her nape with his fingertips.

Sydney shifted a little farther away from him, saying with body language what she hadn't put in words.

"Were you an only child?" he asked after a minute of silence. "Or is that an impolitic question, too?"

"My mother never married, and never had any other dalliances after my father, if that's what you mean. How about you?"

He stuck his tongue in his cheek. "No, I haven't had any dalliances, either."

Sydney's cheeks turned rosy before his eyes. "I meant, do you have any brothers or sisters?"

He laughed. "No, I was an only child, too. And I admit to being spoiled rotten until I was five or six." His smile gleamed. "My critics say I've never recovered."

She laughed. "Are they wrong?"

"What do you think?"

She seemed to struggle a bit with her response. "You do seem to enjoy having your way."

He picked up his drink again and absently swirled the contents. "Do you get the feeling that we seem to talk past each other?"

"You surely aren't accusing *me* of being too subtle," she replied brightly.

He scowled, annoyed that she refused to have a serious conversation with him. "I wasn't thinking so much about the way you talk, as what you choose to say."

"For instance?"

"Your old man was a problem for you, wasn't he?"

Sydney didn't say anything for a minute. Then she sighed. What was it about Zinn Garrett that made him seem to want to come at her from all sides? She felt as though she was constantly under siege. It seemed as if he was either teasing her, touching her, or probing her psyche at every opportunity.

And discussing her father was not something she had any special desire to do. She decided to tell Zinn so. "Could we choose another subject to talk about?"

They each toyed with their glasses, sitting silently, the tension between them growing. The mention of her father had brought an unexpected wave of emotion, and

Sydney felt her eyes begin to mist. She avoided looking at Zinn, hoping it would quickly pass.

"At the risk of opening another can of worms, may I ask a different question?" Zinn said.

She glanced at him apprehensively.

"I'm curious," he began. "Is it actors, or the film industry in general you don't like?"

Sydney gave up. She put down her mineral water and folded her hands in her lap. "Zinn, I don't know how to answer that, except to say that my mother and I have very different feelings about both the film business and the past—her relationship with my father and the circumstances in which I came into the world. Does that answer your question?"

"I'm not Dick Charles, Sydney."

She wasn't sure what he was implying, but she took it as a provocation. "I don't see what my family background has to do with anything. Anyway, I consider it a private matter."

"I withdraw the comment, then."

"Thank you."

"I'm curious, though. What do you know about me, Sydney? About who I really am?"

She was momentarily taken aback. "I haven't made it my business to know anything about you, except what's relevant to the job."

He leaned closer to her, to make his point. "That's all well and good, but we are getting into an area that *is* my business. You've made the point that all that matters in this arrangement is whether or not you can do the job. I grant you that's key. But Andrea's security is a personal thing. Because of that, maybe I take a—I don't know—humanistic view of things. I guess what I'm saying is, I don't want to be misunderstood."

She looked directly at him. "Do I misunderstand you, Zinn?"

He seemed to struggle with his answer. "I get a sense that you don't know me. And what's worse is, I think I'm a victim of your prejudices."

"That's a pretty heavy accusation."

Zinn smiled at her, perhaps to soften his remark—or maybe it was just his instinct to charm that was at work. Sydney didn't know which. But he showed he wasn't going to let a war of words get in his way. He reached out and brushed her cheek with the backs of his fingers, as though he had every right to do so. She kept her eyes on him, and didn't move.

"I wasn't born an actor," he said, seemingly determined to have his say. "As a matter of fact, I never gave it much thought before getting into the business. I don't know if you've heard the story, but I was in law school when I was...discovered." As he pronounced the word, he made quotation signs in the air with his fingers.

"No, I hadn't heard that."

"Yeah. It was my first year. Law seemed a good thing to do. I went into the grind thinking it was the best way to come out the other end of the pipeline with some change in my jeans. Then Lloyd Ferris, a director who also happened to be the father of a classmate of mine, saw me and asked if I'd ever thought about acting. I'd done a little in high school and college—more because it seemed like a good way to meet girls than for any great love of the stage—and took him up on his offer of a screen test."

"And the rest, as they say, is history?" she prompted, trying to keep the sarcasm out of her voice.

"Well, yes. But the point I'm making is Lloyd offered me a chance to make some easy money and have a little fun at the same time. I wasn't an overnight success, but when the Grant Adams job came along, it was soon apparent I could become financially secure to the point that going back to law school would never be necessary."

"Zinn, you don't have to justify yourself to me."

He reached out and lightly touched the edge of her jaw. "Maybe I want to."

Sydney let his words sink in. She tried not to think about his touch, or the fact that he had begun toying with a loose tendril of her hair. "All right," she said. "So you're in it for a profit. I do what I do because I like it."

"Oh, I enjoy my work," he corrected, moving still closer to her. "Don't get me wrong. The benefits are fairly obvious, though the adulation wears thin after a while. And it can be tedious. But I am *not* Grant Adams. I'm me. Only a few friends and colleagues in the business know that, and appreciate what it means. And frankly, I feel really frustrated when people like you refuse to see me for the person I am."

She leaned forward and put her glass on the coffee table. When she sat back, she scooted a few inches farther from him. "Maybe that's the price of fame."

"No. It's why strangers react to me as they do, but it's not reason enough for you to refuse to look beneath the surface."

It was the most serious comment he'd made, and Sydney didn't know what to make of it. A part of her wanted to ask him why it mattered, but another part of her was afraid of the answer.

Zinn moved closer to her again. He casually took her hand, as though he had earned the right. The affection was restrained, and he lightened the moment with a smile. He looked down at her fingers as he played with them, apparently calculating his next words.

Sydney felt the tremor his touch produced work its way down her spine. Their eyes met, and his look took a giant step beyond what he'd said. In the course of just a few minutes, she'd gone from feeling guarded to actually feeling sympathetic toward him—which was probably exactly what Zinn had had in mind. She wasn't sure what he would do next, but before he had a chance to say anything more, Andrea appeared in the doorway.

"Daddy, Daddy! Yolanda says dinner is ready. Now!"

Zinn patted Sydney's hand, as if to indicate he'd decided to let her have it back. Then he turned toward the door and said to Andrea, "I guess that means we have to come to the table, doesn't it?"

"Unless you want everything to get cold."

Scooting to the edge of the cushion, Zinn tweaked Sydney's chin. "That's our first rule around here. Never let anything turn cold."

4

AFTER DINNER ANDREA WENT off with Yolanda to have
her bath. Zinn went to his study to make some phone
calls, and Sydney wandered out into the backyard.
Ostensibly she was going to check the lighting; but as
much as anything, she wanted a breath of air.

It was a pleasant evening. Lights of the city extended
south and east to infinity, forming a gleaming carpet of
glitter that mirrored the stars above. Only to the west,
where the Pacific lay, was there darkness. Pacific Palisades, the last enclave of the privileged before the sea,
sat on the edge of the continent. And Zinn Garrett lived
in its highest reaches—on top of the world, it seemed;
just below the clouds.

As Sydney looked down at the lights of Santa Monica below, she thought about Zinn's rarefied life-style.
He'd made it big, all right. He was making more money
for each weekly episode of *For the Defense* than most
people made in years.

Of course, Hollywood's brand of fame had a way of
treating actors more like meteors than real stars.
Sometimes they would flare up brightly only to burn
out and plunge to earth. The lucky ones socked enough
away during their heydays to live well for the balance
of their lives. Others had to struggle, like the rest of the
human race. But what was the hardest for some was the
loss of glory, the stigma of being a has-been.

Sydney wondered how prepared emotionally Zinn
Garrett was for the decline that only a very few in Hol-

lywood ever escaped. Was there enough else in his life to keep him happy? Strangely, she was worried for him, though didn't know why. What did she care, anyway?

She moved off toward the farthest reaches of the yard. A low wall marked the perimeter of the property. Beyond it the mountain dropped precipitously to the dark canyon below. Sydney sat on the wall and looked back at the house. It was a jewel box lit up like a modern fairy castle against the night sky.

During dinner, odd and unexpected feelings had passed through her. Zinn had sat at one end of the long dining-room table, and Yolanda had placed her at the other. Andrea sat between them, almost as if she were their child. As they ate, bantering with the little girl, Sydney kept thinking of Zinn's apparent concern about how she perceived him. He'd sensed her prejudices and they bothered him—something she wouldn't have expected.

Over the course of the meal Zinn had struck her as rather pleasant. His ego seemed to have receded—invisible acting?—and she actually found him endearing. In Andrea's presence he quickly shifted from the weightier topics they'd discussed when they were alone. He'd asked her about her martial-arts training and the occasions where she'd actually had to employ her skills.

He'd brought Andrea into the discussion, using Sydney's feats to illustrate how self-reliant a woman could be. That struck her as being terribly aware and sensitive to an issue that could only become more important to the child as she grew older.

Even as she appreciated Zinn's comments, Sydney marveled at them. His love for his daughter had been apparent from the outset, but to show such awareness and concern for the development of her self-image was a surprise. Listening to his comments at the dinner table made her wonder all the more about the things he'd said about her unwillingness to acknowledge the man behind the facade.

He'd been right, and he'd correctly discerned the cause of her misgivings. That didn't change the fact of who he was. But it did tell her there might be more complexity to him than she had allowed.

As she sat thinking about him, Zinn appeared at the sliding-glass door accessing the patio. Because of the size of the place, he was easily a hundred and fifty feet away. Sydney was sure he couldn't see her in the dark. Yet, as he moved beyond the pool, his eyes apparently adjusted to the darkness and he spotted her. He meandered her way.

"Nice view, isn't it?" he said, coming near.

Sydney stood and turned around to face the twinkling lights of Los Angeles. "Yes, it's lovely." She hugged her bare arms, though she couldn't exactly say she was cold.

Zinn put his arm around her shoulders in a casual, friendly way. He did it so naturally, so easily, that it was hard to take offense. That invisible acting again, she told herself. Family men behaved that way, and Zinn played the role to perfection. Still, Sydney didn't want him touching her—even innocently. But she let it pass, telling herself she didn't want to offend him.

"What do you think?" he asked. "Will we be able to keep my darling daughter out of harm's way?"

"I don't see why not. We're not dealing with the Cosa Nostra, after all."

"Barbara's pretty terrifying, Sydney—even to me."

His voice was very low and serious. And she was absolutely sure that he wasn't acting.

"What's the story with her, anyway? The newspaper accounts have been kind of vague."

He let out a long sigh. "She's a crazy woman, that's the only way to describe her. She's been obsessed with me for a couple of years now—from when the show first came on the air. And she has a knack for tracking me down." He laughed, squeezing the tip of her shoulder. "Maybe she's a retired P.I."

"Thanks."

"She's managed to pop up at the most unexpected times and places. The worst—apart from this latest incident with Andrea—was in Mexico. I was down in Puerto Vallarta with some friends, staying in the villa Monica and I had when we were married. One evening I wasn't feeling well and left the restaurant we'd all gone to, leaving my friends in town.

"I found Barbara sitting in a chair in my bedroom, naked. I guess she expected me to make love with her. But, to be honest, it scared the hell out of me. Imagine—walking in and finding that waiting!"

"What's she look like?"

"Fairly attractive. She's a redhead. About my age—mid-thirties." He grinned in the dark. "She's well-endowed. I can attest to that."

"What did she do?"

"Mostly she was babbling nonsense. It amounted to now that Monica and I were divorced, she wanted us to get married. I thought maybe she was on drugs, but then again that may be the way she is. I just don't know." He took a deep breath. "There have been other incidents, though not as dramatic. The police have concluded she's nuts, but apparently sharp enough to evade capture."

"And they haven't been able to determine her identity?"

"No. 'Barbara'—the way she refers to herself—is all we know. If I could find out who she is I'd have her arrested, get a restraining order, whatever. Unfortunately she's wily. Slips away as easily as she slips in. I didn't get too upset until she got hold of my unlisted number and called me at home, threatening harm to Andrea if I wouldn't marry her. Even then, I wasn't dead worried—not until that attempt at the supermarket."

"You're sure it's the same woman?"

"The description matched perfectly. Barbara, I'm afraid, has upped the ante."

Zinn stroked Sydney's bare shoulder. She looked at him, trying to decide what he intended by the affection, but he seemed to be doing it unconsciously. He was gazing out at the view, apparently oblivious. Innocent or not, she was very much aware of his hand on her flesh. She trembled and moved away.

"Are you cold?"

"No, not really." She was at the wall and peered out at the sea of lights. Zinn had made her nervous. But it was her reaction to him that troubled her even more.

He was silent behind her for a long time. Finally he spoke. "Are you sorry you took the job?"

Sydney turned around. She started to deny it. Then she was ready to admit it. But she didn't want to blow everything by complaining about his touching her. He hadn't exactly done anything untoward. He was probably just being himself. How could he know how upsetting his effect on her was? The man was from a world she wanted no part of—at least emotionally.

"*Are* there misgivings?" he asked.

Sydney sighed, knowing there was no way she could tell him the truth. And if he'd already figured it out, then all he was looking for was the satisfaction of hearing her admit his attractiveness was a problem to her. That would be typical of an actor. Their egos could be insatiable. She settled on an oblique response. "You assume too much."

"What's that supposed to mean?"

They were about ten feet apart, and his face was in shadow. The light from the house was behind him, silhouetting his body. Despite her desire not to be affected by his physical appeal, she was—much more than was comfortable. "You might be a touchy-feely sort of guy, Zinn, but I don't want a touchy-feely relationship."

He looked puzzled for a moment, then seemed to understand. "That's all?"

"Well, isn't that enough?" She didn't know why she bothered saying it. Maybe he hadn't even touched her consciously.

"I don't think that's it, Sydney."

She turned her back to him. She was almost sure he was talking about her father, and she didn't want to get into a discussion of him again. And yet she knew it wasn't really Zinn's fault. She was being buffeted by the same old emotions that had tormented her for much of her life.

Sydney had hardly seen her father in the early days—only a few times a year and only briefly, sometimes for just several minutes. Her recollections of those encounters were hazy. Her mother had explained it by saying that Dick didn't understand children and didn't relate to them well; that she shouldn't take it personally. But how could she not? After all, he was her father.

If it had been left at that, it probably would have been better. But Lee had made a big mistake when Sydney was twelve. She'd pressured Dick into spending a day with his daughter, to try to get to know her. It had been a disaster.

Afraid to face her alone, he'd had her come to his house when he was entertaining a small group of friends. It was a casual gathering of people out by the pool of his Bel Air home; Sydney was driven up from Glendale in a big black limousine.

She could still see herself in her pink dress and petticoats, her hair and nails done up, completely overdressed and out of place. Dick had greeted her uncertainly, like some sort of museum exhibit that had been dropped off for the party. But when he saw that she was harmless, he'd let himself fall into the role, playing loving father in front of his friends.

Sydney had walked around the grounds with him, meeting people. Dick's hand had often rested on her shoulder, the convivial host and father for a day. He probably hadn't even been aware that those brief touches were the only physical contact she would ever recall having with him.

Even if the performance had been more for the benefit of his friends than for her, it hadn't kept Sydney from falling under his spell. He'd been so charming, she would have forgiven him all his sins. The truth was, she wanted to throw herself in his arms and have him hug her. She'd wanted him to act like a father.

Looking back on it afterward, she'd figured out what had happened. The guy had said to himself, "Dick, this kid is your daughter, which means that for today you're a daddy. Put on your daddy face and get out there and give the performance of your life." She wasn't sure how hard he'd really had to try. The deception might have come as naturally to him as the seduction of whichever woman he'd had that night.

"Hypocrite," she mumbled.

"Pardon?" Zinn moved to her side.

Sydney suddenly realized she'd said it out loud. "Sorry. I was thinking of something else."

"I'd hate to retrace that thought progression," he said, smiling.

"It doesn't have anything to do with you."

"Are you sure about that?"

Sydney looked at him, remembering her father but seeing Zinn. "I was recalling an incident from the past, if you must know. Something involving my father."

"Oh."

"It's nothing. It happens every once in a while."

"But it just happened to happen now." He sounded skeptical.

"Don't try to make anything out of it, Zinn."

"Maybe *you* should try to make something out of it."

She let out a meaningful sigh. "Please, don't try playing shrink. I'm not in the mood."

He took her by the arm. "Sydney, don't always run from it. Say what's on your mind. Let it out."

"It was nothing. A stupid childhood memory."

"Nothing's stupid that upsets you."

She shook her head. "It's really no big deal. I was just remembering the first time I'd spent any meaningful time with my father. I was twelve. It was years ago."

"You were obviously hurt."

She shrugged, trying to hide the pain. "That was the way my father was."

"Tell me about it."

So, Sydney gave up. She told Zinn Garrett about that day in Bel Air, thirteen-odd years before. She told him not only what had happened, but how she felt—how much it had hurt because of how much she had wanted her father's love.

As she talked, rambling on, Zinn put his arm around her shoulders. She leaned against him without really noticing that she was. But when she did notice, she was amazed at how easy it was to fall under his spell, to trust him.

Her father had been as smooth as silk, too. And if he didn't exactly give her what she wanted, he didn't withhold his charm, either. But when she had gotten up the next morning, Sydney had realized it was over — like a movie that had played until the reel ran out. After a brief appearance in her life Dick Charles had gone, and he'd taken the dream with him.

"I never knew your father," Zinn said, "so I can't explain him or understand him. But I can tell you this. There's no comparison between what you've described, and the way I feel about Andrea, for example."

"I'm not comparing. That's not what it's about."

"I think you are, whether you realize it or not. And it just might be true that Dick and I do have some things in common, because of our professions. But that hardly means we're the same kind of people. I'm not Dick Charles."

"You said that before."

Zinn turned her toward him. He took her chin and lifted it so she had to look him in the eye. "And I'll say it over and over again, until you get the point."

"Zinn . . ." She was looking up into his eyes, illuminated by the lights of Los Angeles. His hand had slipped around to the nape of her neck. His fingers were large and warm on her flesh. He was ignoring her wariness and uncertainty, bent, it seemed, on only one thing.

He took her face in his hands, then, and lowered his mouth to hers. And she let him kiss her, dumbly, willingly. It didn't seem to matter that she didn't really want it, that she preferred to let things rest where they were.

Zinn kissed her with a tenderness that impelled her, drawing her deeper into his game. Gently he gathered her body against his. Her breasts pressed against his chest as her lips parted, permitting the kiss to deepen. His tongue slid along her teeth and gently probed her mouth. All the reasons for her reluctance slipped from her mind as easily as she had slipped into his arms. In seconds, the only reality was his embrace.

By then, she had let go. She was in a free-fall, helpless to stop, unwilling to even try. His affection, his lips, sucked her deeper and deeper.

And when his mouth finally separated from hers, it lingered for a moment, touching her lips, brushing them with his warm breath. Sydney luxuriated in the sensation for a long while, aware not only of his kisses, but of his body so forcefully possessing hers.

Finally she opened her eyes to see him, to try to understand what had happened. Zinn was looking at her, waiting for her to look at him. She could feel his chest rising against her, his arms holding her close.

It suddenly occurred to her that she'd done all the things she'd cautioned herself not to do. She'd let herself be swept away. Sydney couldn't even say for sure why it was wrong, but her fear, her past experience, assured her that it was.

Having brought herself back to earth, she gently extricated herself from his arms. With a little distance between them, and safely beyond his magnetic range, she was able to summon a rush of indignity over what had happened. Zinn looked as though he wasn't through, and didn't like her sudden change of heart—which only made her more determined to bring the episode to an end.

Turning abruptly, she started for the house, but Zinn grabbed her wrist.

"Don't!" she protested, pulling away.

"Stay," he said, his tone falling just short of a command.

"I don't want this."

He spoke quietly, in almost a whisper. "*I* do."

She jerked her arm, but he wouldn't let go. She could see she'd have to slug him, or give him a judo toss, if she was to force the issue. But she preferred reason. She let her arm go slack. "Zinn, this isn't why I'm here. And if it's what you have in mind, then I'm going to have to leave."

"You knew I was going to kiss you," he said, his gaze probing hers. "You didn't try to stop me. I'm sorry if you changed your mind, but I don't apologize for it. My intentions weren't bad."

"Your intentions don't matter. I don't want this kind of relationship." Her eyes bored into his. "I really don't!"

He stared at her for a long time, neither acknowledging nor refuting what she'd said. Then he let go of her wrist. Sydney took a step back.

"If you'd like my resignation," she said, "I understand."

"No. To the contrary, you've got to stay. I have a meeting to attend tonight, and I'll be gone for a few hours. I don't want Andrea and Yolanda here alone."

"A meeting?"

"Both my producer and director are night people, and they like to have creative sessions during their creative times. It happens once every two or three months, and tonight is it. The point is, I need to know Andrea will be all right. Since the kidnapping attempt, I haven't left the house in the evening."

"Okay. I'll stay, then. At least for tonight."

They looked into each other's eyes for a moment, then she turned to go.

"Wait," he said.

She stopped.

"I'm not sorry I kissed you. And, if you're really honest, I don't think you can say you're sorry, either."

Sydney didn't reply to his comment. She walked to the house, her gait becoming more brisk with each step.

SYDNEY HAD CHANGED INTO her L.A. Dodgers T-shirt, which she always slept in, and sat cross-legged in the middle of the bed. The goose bumps on her arms hadn't gone away, though it had been half an hour since Zinn had left. His kiss still affected her—there was no denying that. How silky-smooth he'd been. And how easily she'd fallen. Sydney rolled over and pounded her fist into the pillow. How could she have been so stupid?

She was more upset with herself than with Zinn. Worse, she was embarrassed. All those years she'd marveled that her mother could have been taken in so easily by an actor, and here she was, being manipulated in much the same way. Of course, a kiss fell quite a bit short of a love affair and an illegitimate child, but every relationship had to start somewhere.

She got up and began pacing around the room. She made a halfhearted attempt to convince herself that what Zinn had done practically amounted to sexual harassment, but she knew that simply wasn't true. She had been as much at fault as him. In the future it would be up to her to keep things businesslike.

After a while she lay down and stared at the ceiling. She listened to the quiet in the house and tried to concentrate on the little girl she'd been hired to protect. That was the problem, actually. She'd let Zinn's appeal distract her, when all she had to do was keep her mind on the job. It had been unprofessional to permit him to get to her the way she had—especially when she'd been warned to expect that sort of thing from him. Actors thrived on adoring women; she'd known that for years.

Well, maybe it wasn't too late. If she kept her mind on her work she'd be all right. Taking her robe, Sydney went down the hall to Andrea's room to look in on her charge. A night-light cast a soft glow around the room. She went over to the bed and peered down at the girl's angelic face. She was a precious child. What a tragedy that her safety was threatened simply because of her father's fame.

As she stared at the sleeping girl, she thought of her own childhood—her heartache in having a father who wouldn't acknowledge her and love her like a daughter. Thinking about Dick Charles while looking at Zinn's little girl brought tears to her eyes, and she turned to leave the room. But she only got as far as the door before stopping and looking back again.

The past had a way of living on in the form of adult resentment of childhood unhappinesses. But Andrea was lucky in one sense: Zinn seemed genuinely to love her—which was more than could have been said for her own father. So why did she have such a strong emotional reaction to Zinn? Maybe because he was, in his own way, as irresistible as her father had once been?

It took a while for Sydney to fall asleep that night, but she finally did. Her dreams, which came immediately, were full of anxiety. She was thrashing about in her sleep when a hand shook her awake. She looked up into a face above her—a woman's face with eyes as wide as her own. The sound in Sydney's throat fell just short of a scream.

"Señorita, señorita!" came the breathless voice. "There is someone. I am very frightened."

Only then did Sydney realize the face she was staring at was Yolanda's. She lifted herself to her elbows. "Who? What are you saying?"

"Outside," the housekeeper said in an anxious whisper. "There is someone outside. I turn off my television after Jay Leno, he say good-night. Then I turn off my light. And outside my window I see someone. I am very afraid. It is this Barbara. I am sure."

Sydney threw back the covers and got out of bed. She picked up the 9-mm semiautomatic on the bedside table.

"Oh, Holy Mother," Yolanda intoned at the sight of the gun, crossing herself.

Sydney took the woman's arm. "Did you see her clearly? Are you sure it was Barbara?"

"Not her face, no. But who else could it be, *señorita?"*

"A burglar, I suppose. Don't worry, Yolanda, I'll take care of it." She could feel the woman trembling. "I want you to go into Andrea's room and wait there while I check it out. If someone besides me comes in, start yelling at the top of your lungs."

"Sí, señorita. This I can do."

Sydney went to the telephone by the bed.

"What you do now?"

"I'm calling the police."

Yolanda crossed herself again and stole silently from the room. Sydney dialed 911 and gave the dispatcher the address and a brief description of the problem. Then she went into the hallway. The house was dark. She wondered what time it was, and whether Zinn had returned. She crept along the hall toward the master suite.

Yolanda had said she'd just finished watching Jay Leno. That put the time somewhere around twelve-thirty. As she passed Andrea's room, Sydney looked in and saw the housekeeper in the dim light, sitting on a chair next to the sleeping child. Her head was bowed, her hands were folded in her lap. She appeared to be praying.

Sydney continued along the corridor until she arrived at Zinn's room. The door was open, but it was too dark to see clearly. She inched her way inside, her finger resting nervously on the trigger guard of the gun. By the time she got to the bed, she could see it was still made. Apparently Zinn wasn't home.

Just then she saw motion out of the corner of her eye. Her heart leaped. Turning quickly, she saw a figure outside, going past the window frame. She had only a glimpse—not enough to identify the nature of the apparition. Sydney could feel her heart race.

Whoever it was seemed to be circling the house methodically. Yolanda's room was at the other end of the structure, near the kitchen. Judging by the direction of movement, the person had come around the front of the house and was progressing toward the rear, perhaps looking for an open window or door.

Fingering the gun, Sydney left the master suite and slipped back along the hallway. A glance into Andrea's room told her Yolanda was still fervently engaged in prayer. Sydney crept through the living room, catching a glimpse of the shadowy figure outside in the shrubs before it disappeared from sight.

Next she entered the solarium, which accessed the patio. The stalker would be coming here if she had guessed right. Sydney's mouth was dry, her breathing staccato. She squeezed the handle of the gun and hid in the shadows.

She saw movement in the foliage at the edge of the patio. Before the figure emerged, a loud buzzing sound broke the silence. Sydney jumped.

The sound was the intercom at the security gate. It was probably the police. She stole quickly to the entry hall, where the central control system was. Pushing the intercom, she heard the voice of a police officer.

"There's an intruder," she said into the speaker. "A moment ago he was in the shrubs off the patio behind the house."

The officer acknowledged and Sydney pushed the release button, activating the security gate. Adrenaline was coursing through her veins as she hurried back toward the solarium. Entering the room, she ran smack into someone in the darkness. She screamed.

The figure recoiled. Instinctively Sydney swung her gun hand, catching the intruder on the side of the head with the weapon. The figure collapsed at her feet.

She jumped back, aiming the gun at the prone form. "Freeze!" she shouted. There was no movement, no sound apart from the pounding of her own heart. Keeping the gun aimed at the motionless heap, she backed to the doorway, searching the wall with one hand for the light switch. The room suddenly filled with harsh light.

Sydney squinted at the figure—a man. Taking a step forward, she took a look at his face. Her mouth sagged open. It was Zinn Garrett!

"Oh, my God!" She knelt beside him, eyeing the stream of blood flowing across his temple and down his cheek. "Zinn, I'm so sorry! I had no idea it was you."

As she touched his face, he groaned. She heaved a sigh of relief. For a moment she'd thought she had killed him. He groaned again and his eyelids fluttered. Sydney lifted his head onto her lap. She felt tears welling in her eyes.

"Zinn, please forgive me."

There was a sound at the doorway and she looked up to see a police officer, his gun drawn.

"You all right, miss?"

"Yes."

"That's the intruder?"

Sydney nodded, biting her lip to keep from crying. "I thought he was an intruder. He isn't. He lives here. This is his house."

The policeman holstered his weapon as a second officer came running onto the patio behind him. The two of them entered the house. "Who are you?" the first asked.

"Sydney Charles. I'm a P.I. Mr. Garrett here hired me to provide security."

The officer smiled. "You certainly did that." He knelt down to look at Zinn's head. "He took a good whack, Eddie," the policeman said to his partner. "Better call for medical assistance."

The second officer used the radio he carried on his belt to request an ambulance and report developments to the dispatcher. He stepped toward the open doorway as he talked.

Sydney was still holding Zinn's head. His blood was dripping onto her bare knee. He was mumbling semi-coherently. She looked up at the cop, who had knelt beside them.

"Head wounds can bleed pretty heavily," he told her. "I wouldn't worry about the blood so much as his brains. He seems a little scrambled."

Zinn was rolling his eyes and muttering something about Barbara. Sydney stroked his cheek.

"I'm so sorry," she said over and over.

The officer picked up the gun lying on the floor. "This what you hit him with?"

She nodded, biting her lip.

"You're licensed?"

"Yes."

"Don't suppose you have an ID."

"In my room. Do you want me to get it?"

The officer's brow furrowed. "You live here?"

"I moved in today."

Zinn was mumbling again, trying to lift his head. "Andrea? Andrea?"

"She's fine, Zinn. Andrea's fine."

"You just relax, sir," the cop said. "We'll have medical assistance here soon. Just take it easy."

Zinn put his hand to his bleeding head and sat up, despite their words. He looked back and forth between Sydney and the policeman. He appeared coherent for the first time, having come out of it. "What happened?"

"The lady here thought you were an intruder."

Zinn tried to focus on Sydney. "*You* clobbered me?"

She nodded. "I didn't know it was you."

He took a handkerchief from his pocket and pressed it to the side of his head where her blow had split the skin like a ripe melon. "Remind me to announce my arrival with a fanfare, from now on."

Sydney grimaced. "Why didn't you use your key and come in the front door?"

Zinn winced. "I was testing the security."

She shook her head. "I believe it works."

He grinned lamely.

"Can I assume this was an accident, then?" the officer asked.

"More like a case of gross stupidity on my part," Zinn moaned.

The sound of a distant siren wafted in the open door. "Ambulance will be here in a minute," the cop by the door said. "I'll meet them at the gate."

Zinn tried to get up, but the policemen restrained him. "Better stay right where you are, sir. Let the paramedics look at you. Head injuries can be tricky."

Sydney took the handkerchief from Zinn and wiped his cheek and neck. "Your shirt's ruined."

Despite his condition he managed to drag his gaze down her body. She was still kneeling beside him, and when he saw the blood on her knee, he wiped it away with his hand. Then he poked her lower thigh with his finger. "This what you wear to bed?"

Sydney colored at his question. She glanced down at her T-shirt. In her anxiety over Zinn's injury, she'd forgotten all about the way she was dressed. Outside, the siren had died. The officer, sensing her uneasiness, volunteered to let the paramedics in the front door. Sydney pointed the way.

When the policeman was gone, Zinn reached over and touched her fiery cheek with his hand. "Guess I don't have to wonder whether you're tough enough for this job anymore."

She bit her lip. "You aren't angry?"

"I haven't decided." Then he smiled. "Maybe I can find a way for you to make it up to me."

About then, the paramedics and the two police officers came in. The medics immediately set about examining Zinn.

"All I need is an aspirin and a bandage," he told them.

"Looks to me like you won't get off quite that cheap, mister," one paramedic, a young man, said. "We'd better have a doctor look at that head of yours."

"You don't know one who does house calls, do you?"

The man laughed. "You'd better hope there'll be one willing to go to the emergency room. This ain't like the old days, mister."

"Yeah," Zinn said under his breath. "When women were women and men were men."

Sydney self-consciously pulled down on her T-shirt, which only came to mid-thigh. The front of Zinn's shirt was soaked with blood, and the floor was spattered, too. She watched, feeling terrible.

The paramedics made Zinn lie down, and had rolled the stretcher in. They prepared, with the aid of the police officers, to lift him onto the stretcher.

Sydney felt awful. She would have volunteered to ride with him to the hospital, but knew she couldn't leave Andrea.

"I'll be home as soon as I get my aspirin and my bandage, and see these boys are paid," Zinn said to her. He extended his hand and she stepped over to him. He held her fingers, squeezing them.

Sydney pressed his hand to her cheek. "I really am sorry."

Zinn smiled. "It was almost worth it."

"Does it hurt terribly?"

"This is one time I don't have to act."

"Ready, mister?" the paramedic asked.

"Ready as I'll ever be."

They wheeled him out and Sydney followed them to the door. After Zinn had been loaded into the ambulance, they took off. One of the police officers stood next to her, watching until the ambulance had cleared the gate.

"Now, if you don't mind, ma'am, I'd like to see your ID and get a little information for my report."

"I'll go get my purse." Sydney headed back toward her room. In the hallway she saw Yolanda peering out of the door of Andrea's room.

"Did you shoot a criminal, *señorita?*"

"Not exactly, Yolanda. I sort of shot myself in the foot."

5

THE NEXT MORNING, after an early breakfast, Sydney went with Andrea to the hospital in Zinn's car. She was a little apprehensive about seeing him. Entering the house in the dark the way he had may have been a foolish thing to do, and under the circumstances Sydney couldn't be blamed; but it didn't stop her from feeling badly.

Worst of all, the incident had changed the psychological balance between them; now she felt an obligation to show compassion. Zinn had been an unwary victim who'd suffered at her hand. Would he use her guilt over that against her? She didn't know.

He was propped up in bed looking bright-eyed and alert when they appeared at his door. "There they are!" he said cheerfully.

Andrea shrieked gleefully and ran to her father. He reached over and pulled her into his arms. They exchanged big wet kisses as Sydney made her way over to the bed. While Andrea hugged him, he glanced up at Sydney.

"Good morning."

He looked good to her—more benign in a hospital setting—but underneath it all, perhaps more threatening because of the guilt she felt. There was a bandage on the side of his face next to his hairline, and some swelling. Otherwise there wasn't a thing to indicate he'd run into a chunk of steel the night before.

"How are you feeling?"

He grinned. "Like I've got a hangover with no fun to show for it."

"Do you want my resignation?" Sydney tried to keep her voice even and controlled, but it was all she could do to keep from holding her breath.

Andrea was sitting up beside her father and playing with the plastic ID bracelet on his wrist. He stroked her hair, which Yolanda had again fixed into a single braid like Sydney's. "To the contrary, I'm considering giving you a raise. If I'd been a bad guy, I'd have wanted you to do exactly what you did."

He extended his hand toward her and Sydney inched close enough for him to touch her. He rubbed her fingers affectionately with his thumb. She knew it was the wrong thing to be doing, but she told herself she didn't want to offend him, considering. . . .

"I shouldn't have been sneaking around the way I was," Zinn said with a glance at Andrea, "but I was feeling a little paranoid and wanted to check out the house."

"Why?"

"On my way home from my meeting, I believe I was being followed."

Sydney, too, looked over at Andrea to make sure she wasn't paying attention to their conversation. "Followed? By you-know-who?"

"I don't know, but I thought it was a possibility."

"Did you get a good look at the car? A license plate? Anything?"

"No. I tried, but she kept her distance."

"Daddy," Andrea said, growing impatient, "are you coming home?"

"Yes, angel. Right after the doctor comes to see me."

"Are you sick?"

He glanced at Sydney. "Let's say I bumped my head."

"How come?"

He gave Sydney's hand a firm squeeze. "I guess I fell for someone, angel."

Sydney groaned.

"Yes," he admitted. "That was a bad one."

"What does that mean?" Andrea asked.

"Nothing. Just a little joke."

"Very little," Sydney added. But she was feeling better. She pulled her hand free. He'd been indulged enough.

A nurse came to the door. "The doctor will be in to see you in a few minutes," she said. "I'm afraid your family will have to wait for you in the visitors' lounge."

Zinn caught Sydney's eye. "You see, darling. Word of a relationship travels fast in this town. We make a commitment, have our first tiff, make up. Next thing you know it'll be in all the gossip columns, blown completely out of proportion."

Sydney felt her cheeks flame.

"Don't worry, though," he went on. "I'll have my publicist put out the usual denials. She'll insist that we're as happy as a couple of clams." Zinn laughed and Sydney was so embarrassed that she could have slugged him.

But amid the joking an idea occurred to her. And she realized it would fit into their plans perfectly.

"I'll give you a few more minutes," the nurse told them, making a discreet withdrawal.

"Zinn," Sydney said, growing so excited she could hardly contain herself, "I know you were kidding— what you said just now about your publicist—but I think it's a terrific idea. I think you should do it!"

He looked at her like she was crazy. "What are you talking about?"

Sydney glanced at Andrea, who was distracted, looking at the pictures in a magazine Zinn had been reading. "Remember when I told you I thought it would be a good idea to transfer Barbara's hostility to me? That my plan was to draw her out?"

"Yes . . ."

"Well, this is the perfect opportunity to do that. You've been hospitalized—that's newsworthy. We might as well spin out the tale. Like you say, have your publicist report that you'd had an altercation with your live-in lover, that we've kissed and made up and that we're happy as can be. It'll make good press and Barbara is sure to see it." She beamed happily. "With any luck, it'll incite her against me."

"Wonderful. She might shoot you. Then where would we be?"

"Don't be silly, Zinn. I can take care of myself."

He took hold of her hand again and rubbed the back of it with his thumb. "Well, I admit that when you were going over the part about us having made up and being all lovey-dovey, it sounded pretty good."

Sydney extricated her hand once more. "It's only for effect—part of the story we're putting out for public consumption. Our actual relationship has got to be professional, nothing more. I intend for this live-in lover business to be a charade, an act. You of all people ought to be able to understand that."

"Sarcasm," he retorted mildly.

She nodded. "You're right. It was sarcastic. I apologize."

Zinn stroked Andrea's head, but he kept his eyes on Sydney. "If you're going to take on additional danger, it's only fair you be compensated. I'm increasing your salary an extra two hundred a day—hazardous-duty pay."

The nurse reappeared. "I'm sorry, miss, the doctor will be here momentarily. Would you come with me, please?"

Sydney picked up Andrea, who refused to go until Zinn gave her a kiss goodbye. "I appreciate the raise," she said, "but I'm not sure which hazard I'm being compensated for—you-know-who or *you*."

Zinn Garrett grinned. "Maybe I'll keep you guessing."

ZINN AWOKE AFTER DOZING for an hour or so and looked at the afternoon sun coming in his bedroom window. The whack he'd taken on the head had been a little more debilitating than he'd thought, and after lunch he had gone to bed for a short nap.

But first, as soon as they'd arrived home from the hospital, he'd called his publicist, Judy Meecham, and outlined the story of his affair with Sydney, and their fight and reconciliation. Judy found the episode delightful. He didn't bother to tell her the idea had come from Sydney, and that it was only half factual—he figured there was no point in dampening Judy's enthusiasm.

After the call, he'd told Sydney everything was in the works. She'd been pleased, almost gleeful. While he sat in his favorite chair in the den with Andrea on his lap, Sydney had paced the floor, ideas and strategies coming out of her head like a woman possessed. She was clearly dedicated to her work, and on a crusade. In fact, she hadn't bothered to have lunch with them, asking if they'd be all right alone so that she could drive downtown and meet with Marvin Kaslow at the L.A.P.D., to get up to speed on the investigation.

Zinn didn't object, telling her to take his Jaguar. Even though he wasn't feeling up to snuff, he felt Andrea was safe enough as long as he was in the house. So Sydney had bounced out the door, waving goodbye to them all, her braid flying, the purse containing her semiautomatic pistol tucked under her arm.

Zinn sat up in bed, fluffing his pillow behind him. He tried to ignore the dull pain in his head. The otherwise gruesome experience of having been thumped on the noggin did give him a certain amount of confidence in Sydney's abilities. If there was anything about the woman that still bothered him, it was how easily she'd slipped from his arms the night before.

Of course, a great deal couldn't be made of a kiss— not anymore. But in the backyard, with the lights of the city spread out below them, they'd done a lot more than kiss—they'd connected. He'd felt it, and he had no doubt that Sydney had, as well. True, she'd kind of pulled herself together and repudiated him, but he didn't believe her change of heart was sincere. He knew women well enough to know when they were following their hearts, and when they were following their heads.

It was damned disconcerting that so many women nowadays felt guilty whenever their hearts held sway. And that wasn't sexist. He'd always believed men were innately more romantic than women. But it seemed that modern women were consumed with guilt whenever they failed to do what their heads told them was wise.

Sydney Charles was so determined to be taken seriously as a detective that it was like an article of faith to her. "I shouldn't kiss you," she seemed to be telling him, "because I'm a detective." So what!

Zinn pinched the bridge of his nose and tried to relax so that the throbbing would let up. It was a mistake to get himself worked up right now. He didn't want to be unfair to Sydney. The problem was that he'd been through something similar with Monica, and in the end it had cost them their marriage.

The comparison probably wasn't just, but his life experience wasn't easy to ignore—especially in the area of love. Over lunch one day he'd told Patti Lind, the actress he worked with on the show and a close friend, that he thought modern women's independence was often nothing more than an excuse for rejecting husbands and lovers. Patti angrily took exception, accusing him of wanting to keep women submissive and at home—the old barefoot-and-pregnant argument. But he explained that women having careers wasn't the issue; it was when they used their careers as a means to avoid intimacy and keep men at bay. Men did it, too, he argued; and when they did, it was just as wrong.

Zinn heard his bedroom door open and he looked over to see Andrea's face peeking in.

"Daddy, how's your 'cussion?"

He smiled at her, holding out his hand. "My concussion is just fine. Come over here and give your daddy a kiss."

She dashed over and jumped on the bed beside him. Yolanda appeared in the open door.

"We not too sure if you were awake, *señor.*"

"I'm awake and feeling fine."

"Good."

"Any word from Sydney?" he asked.

"Yes. She came home from the police a while ago. I tell her you were sleeping. She wants to talk to you sometime."

"Have her come in now. I'm sure she's seen a man in his pajamas before."

"*Sí, señor.*"

He bussed Andrea on the cheek. "How about if you go with Yolanda, angel face? I'm going to talk to Sydney now."

"Can't I talk to her, too?"

"Not now. Daddy has to talk to her alone. Later, when we're through, you can bring in your checkerboard and we'll play a game."

Andrea jumped down, excited. "Oh, boy! Checkers!" She looked at him, shaking her head. "You won't have a chance, Daddy-do."

He laughed and sent her on her way. A couple of minutes later Sydney knocked softly on the door and entered.

"Well, if it isn't the house detective! How goes the hunt?"

"Terrific." Sydney made her way into the room. She was wearing buff-colored pants that were pleasantly snug around the hips, and a short-sleeved peach blouse. Her golden braid wrapped around her neck and fell between her breasts. The sight of her sent a little twinge through him. The attraction he felt for her was growing by the hour.

He patted the bed, inviting her to sit. He could see by the glow in her cheeks that, in her case, "the thrill of the hunt" was more than just an expression. "What did Kaslow have to say?"

"They haven't accomplished much, which is not a surprise. Barbara's not exactly a serial killer."

"A child was nearly kidnapped. That ought to count for something."

"Oh, they're working on it. But you're wise to have your own detective on the case."

He smiled. "Is that an objective opinion?"

"No, it's self-serving. But that's okay. I already have the job."

Zinn would have liked to reach out and give her braid a tug, but he restrained himself. Actually, he would have liked to give her a kiss, but this was a professional discussion, and she wouldn't have appreciated it. "So, why the euphoria?"

"While I was in the Glass House, Kaslow—"

"Glass House?" Zinn repeated, interrupting.

"Headquarters."

"Oh. Police jargon. I see."

"It's what they call the place. It's not really jargon. Anyway, Kaslow sent me over to the police psychologist who's been reviewing the file. I got a lot of good insights. I think my plan to draw Barbara to me is a sound one. The guy agreed it had a fair chance of working."

"I wish I could get as excited about incipient violence."

Sydney gave him a look. "This is what you hired me for, remember?"

He wanted to tell her he wished he hadn't. He'd much rather be relating to her as a man to a woman, but he knew that wouldn't be appreciated, either. The truth was, it frustrated him that she was so determined to keep him at a distance. With each feint he made, she responded with a straight arm.

What was he doing, falling for a private investigator who hated actors, anyway? He could probably have his pick of a number of women who were much more compliant than Sydney Charles. The problem was, he was interested in Sydney.

In spite of himself, he reached over and took her hand. Her flesh was cooler than his, and he wondered if the rest of her body was like that, too. "Well, I know you're anxious to get on with your plans, but you can't be on duty twenty-four hours a day. Everyone needs some time off," he said.

She stared at his hand, but she didn't pull away. "I'm fine."

"Sure. But you need a private life, too—for friendship, family. . . maybe even a little romance. It's the American way."

Zinn watched her face carefully. She didn't react to his suggestion of needing time for a love life. Of course, she had said that she wasn't currently involved with anyone. But before he could decide what her nonreaction meant, she slid her hand from his and got to her feet.

"I'll let you know if I need any time off, okay? Why don't we talk about it later on." She smiled sweetly and stole from the room.

He watched her carefully shut the door. Then he sighed. Why was he always attracted to difficult women? If he was smart, he'd put a stop to it right now. He'd let her do her job and go home so they each could get on with their lives. But then he shook his head. It wasn't in his nature to let things happen that way. If he did nothing else, he'd get to the bottom of his feelings for her, and, just as important, to the bottom of her feelings for him.

SYDNEY WAS UP VERY EARLY the next morning, before anyone else. She went down to the gate to get the morning paper and installed herself at the kitchen table with a cup of instant coffee. Zinn's publicist had done her job. There was a brief news story on page three about Zinn's injury and hospitalization, and the gossip columns were full of juicy tidbits about a lovers' quarrel and reconciliation. Sydney was identified as the illegitimate daughter of the late Dick Charles—a point that didn't please her—but she had to admit it did add to the prurient interest of the story. Besides, they definitely didn't want it known that she was a private investigator.

After a while Yolanda came in to fix breakfast. She greeted Sydney cheerfully and set about her work.

"Is Zinn an early riser, or does he usually sleep in?" Sydney asked the housekeeper.

"Usually he gets up very early, *señorita*. The shooting starts first thing at the studio. Today he won't go in, he tell me. He must get better, because in a few days they go to location in San Francisco."

"Oh?"

"*Sí, señorita*. And one thing more. Last night Señor Garrett, he ask me to say to you there will be a lunch for you and him at the Hard Rock Café today. The publicity lady, she call last night to tell Señor Garrett the photographers are coming to see the beautiful new girlfriend. This doesn't make sense to me, but he say you understand."

Sydney nodded. "Yes, I do."

"And somebody name Jack will come to stay with the *niña* and me while you are gone."

"Yes, that makes sense."

Yolanda shrugged and went back to her work.

It seemed Zinn's publicist wasn't letting the grass grow under her feet. This romance between them was rapidly becoming a cause célèbre. The thought struck Sydney that she might have created a monster.

Since their kiss, Zinn had been fairly low-key. But there was no doubt in her mind that he was attracted to her. She had felt a strong connection between them from the very first. The question now was, could she forget about that attraction and keep to the hands-off policy that she herself had insisted on?

Not much had happened the previous evening. Zinn had come to the dinner table, trying to be chipper, but it was obvious he wasn't feeling up to par. The doctor had told him a day in bed wouldn't hurt, so he'd gone back to his room after dessert. Andrea had watched a Disney movie with him on the VCR in his bedroom, but Yolanda said Zinn had dozed through most of it.

Sydney had spent her evening planning. She'd called a lighting contractor that Candy Gonzalez used and discussed the security situation with him. The man had agreed to come out for a look that morning and to make recommendations.

Sydney checked her watch. She still had time before the contractor was due. Yolanda brought her a plate of *huevos rancheros,* apparently so pleased Sydney had enjoyed them the previous morning that she'd decided to serve them again.

"I take it Zinn is sleeping in this morning," she said to the housekeeper.

"Yes. He say if he's not awake by nine I must knock on the door. Very busy day."

Sydney had just finished her eggs when the contractor buzzed at the gate. She took a hurried last sip of coffee and went down to meet him. The man, who was a Latino of about sixty named Manny Ibáñez, walked the perimeter of the property with her, pointing out the deficiencies. Sydney asked him for a cost estimate on a quick job that would bring the system up to minimum standards. He promised to call her with a figure that afternoon.

When the contractor had gone, Sydney returned to the house. Zinn was up and breakfasting on the patio. She went out to join him.

"How are you feeling?"

He put down his coffee cup and gave her the old familiar Zinn Garrett smile. "Much better, thanks. I'm a new man. Sit down. Join me."

She was in jeans and a T-shirt. Zinn took it all in as she settled into the chair across from him.

"Did Yolanda tell you about our date for lunch?"

"She said we were going to the Hard Rock Café."

"Judy thought it'd be a good place to make an appearance. Mix and mingle with the public a bit. There'll be some press there."

"To take pictures?"

"Yes, and to see us in action." Zinn took a bite of toast and grinned.

Sydney's eyes narrowed. "In action? What do you mean, 'in action'?"

He swallowed, gesturing with his hands. "You know, the Hollywood date scene. There *are* certain expectations."

"We're going to have lunch together. What else could we do in public?"

"Syd, honey, we're an item now. You know...in love. All we have to do is act like it. A little kissing, mugging for the cameras. No big deal. We've got to be believable."

She stared at him as he sipped his coffee.

"What's the matter, babe?"

"Zinn, why do I feel you're taking advantage of the situation?"

His face was the picture of innocence. "I don't know. Why do you?"

"Because I think you actually like the idea."

He gave her a half smile. "What am I supposed to do, hate the prospect of kissing you? As I recall, it wasn't so bad the other night when we were doing it naturally."

She turned crimson. "You *are* taking advantage!"

"Syd, this was your idea, not mine. I'm simply going along. But there's no point in playing a role halfheartedly. If we're going to get Barbara jealous, let's do it right."

Her eyes narrowed. "As long as you remember it's just an act."

Zinn leaned back in his chair, his gaze leveled on her. "I can't promise you I won't enjoy it. The truth is, I've become rather fond of you. It won't be a difficult role to play."

Sydney got up. "Well, I regard it as a purely professional matter. I hope you have the decency to respect that."

"Certainly."

She started for the door.

"Oh, Syd," he called to her.

She stopped. "Yes?"

"Wear something real sexy and provocative. This is kind of the opening shot of the campaign, and we've got to capitalize on it. The news value will diminish rapidly. Judy suggested we pull out all the stops."

She folded her arms across her chest. "Maybe I should plan on doing a striptease on the table. Do you think that would please Judy?"

Zinn shook his head with mock seriousness. "No, that might be a little too much."

Sydney turned on her heel and marched into the house.

BY ELEVEN, SYDNEY WAS waiting for Jack Dowd in Zinn's huge living room. The twin overstuffed sofas were white, apparently not to compete with all the art. The paintings were colorful modern geometrics. She was fairly certain that one was a Frank Stella. And there was a kinetic sculpture on the coffee table. The plan was for them to leave as soon as Jack arrived, but neither the bodyguard nor Zinn himself had showed up.

Sydney had decided not to let Zinn's ribbing get to her. Although she wasn't a professional actress, she was more than capable of putting on a little show to deceive Barbara. So she had let herself get into the spirit of the thing.

After she'd washed her hair, she'd let it hang down her back, though she'd clipped one side back behind her ear. Her shortest skirt, a white linen number, was a little too respectable, so she'd had Yolanda help her raise the hem to mid-thigh. To that she'd added a red silk tank top, which she wore braless. If Zinn Garrett wanted "sexy," he was going to get "sexy."

She was pacing the living room in her strappy red high-heeled sandals when the doorbell rang. Jack Dowd had the gate code, so she assumed it was the security man. Since Yolanda was in back with Andrea, Sydney answered the door. Dowd was about six-eight and built like a middle linebacker for the Los Angeles Rams. He had wavy dark hair, and was about forty. "Intimidating" was as good a way to describe him as any.

He checked out the miniskirt in as unsubtle a way as a man could. "New upstairs maid?"

"No, downstairs security. I'm Sydney Charles. You must be Dowd."

"Yeah." Judging by his behavior, he liked the silk chemise, too.

Sydney extended her hand. "Forgive the disguise, I'm supposed to be alluring for a photo occasion to draw out our prey."

After shaking her hand, Dowd stepped inside and closed the door. He scratched his head. "I thought the kidnapper was supposed to be a broad. This looks like the wrong disguise to me. If you were standing outside a bank, ten cops wouldn't notice it was being robbed."

Sydney smiled. "Thanks, I guess. This is what Zinn wanted."

Dowd grinned. "I don't blame him." He took long enough to glance around. "Security system still stink?"

"It's pretty basic."

"I told Garrett a long time ago he ought to beef it up."

"I've started on the lighting."

"It's something, but there are limits to what can be done, I guess. The neighbors probably wouldn't like gun towers and spots on all night."

"No, I don't think they would."

Dowd nodded.

"Zinn will be along any minute. Then we'll be taking off."

Jack shrugged his shoulders. "Don't worry about me. I've been here before. I'll just make myself at home." He headed for the kitchen, and probably the refrigerator.

Sydney returned to the front room and sat on a sofa. She looked down at her skirt that ended a good ten inches above her knee. She wondered if, in her exuberance, she hadn't gone a little too far.

Zinn came in after a few minutes. He had on a blue blazer and open-necked pale-yellow shirt. When he saw her, he stood still and stared.

Sydney popped up from the sofa. "Ready?"

His mouth was almost hanging open as he watched her make her way across the room. She stopped in front of him, looking almost defiantly into his eyes. Zinn took half a step back and surveyed her. "Sydney, you definitely look like a woman who could clunk a guy on the head and have him coming back for more."

"Isn't this what you wanted?"

His eyes roamed over her delightedly. "Yes, but I didn't . . . imagine anything this . . . this . . ."

"This what?"

"Devastating. It's perfect."

She tried not to look too self-satisfied. "As you said, today's our best shot."

"Who knows, you might get the paparazzi salivating for more. You could be hounded for weeks."

"No way. One day of this is all you get."

Zinn nodded approvingly. "Did I hear Jack arriving earlier?"

"Yeah, he's in the kitchen."

"Good. That's fine." He wasn't paying any attention to his own words. He seemed more intent on staring.

His reaction almost made her laugh. But when he reached out, hooked a hank of her hair with his fingers and began toying with it, she froze. He moved a bit closer. Then he lifted her chin and kissed her on the lips. Briefly. Sweetly.

"You taste as good as you look," he muttered.

She backed away, forcing a frown of displeasure. "That's not part of the deal."

"Any actor will tell you it takes preparation to get into a role. I'm trying to set a mood, Syd. Purely a professional consideration."

"Yeah, well, keep your hands to yourself until we're amid the press and your adoring public."

"Sydney, I know you're tough as nails, but isn't there a little part of you that enjoyed that?"

She had to struggle to keep from smiling. "I never disclose professional secrets." With that, she went and got her purse from the hall table, then headed for the door. "Who's driving, boss? You or me?"

ZINN HAD HER DRIVE, which Sydney decided was probably a mistake. He spent the whole time looking at her. She tried to keep the conversational ball rolling, but he seemed far more interested in brushing wisps of hair off her cheek, or running his fingertips over the tip of her bare shoulders. He did manage to hold it to that, however.

She told him about the lighting contractor who had come by that morning, and the possibility that some upgrading of the system might be desirable. Zinn compliantly took it in.

"Yolanda mentioned you'll be going on location to San Francisco soon," she remarked.

"Yes. The entire crew's going up for a few days of shooting."

"I've been thinking about it. Might be a good idea if I went along. Particularly if we can publicize it. I'd be really visible, out in the open. Barbara might see it as an opportunity to create some problems and do some dirty work."

"You mean try to hurt you, don't you?"

"*Try* being the operative word, Zinn. My intent is to provoke her into action. And the sooner the better."

Sydney had followed San Vicente Boulevard to Wilshire, across the San Diego Freeway to Westwood, where they stopped at a red light.

"Naturally, I'd love to have you along," he agreed.

"On a strictly professional basis," she cautioned.

"Sydney, you're much too hard-nosed about that," he said, toying with her hair again. "I wish you'd ease up a little."

The light changed and she took off again. "I'm being prudent."

"Then you admit you're tempted."

She gave him a sidelong glance. "Of course I am. You're not chopped liver, Zinn. I'm not too proud to admit that."

He let out an audible sigh. "Thank you. I was beginning to think I'd lost my touch."

"I'll let you know if you do," she replied with a laugh.

They drove through Beverly Hills on Santa Monica Boulevard, turning on Beverly until they came to the shopping center where the Hard Rock Café was located. Sydney pointed to the Cadillac car protruding from the roof in camp fashion as she pulled up at the curb. "I hope that's not an omen," she said.

There were a number of people outside the entrance. Zinn had just reached over and taken the keys from the ignition when a photographer emerged from the crowd and began snapping pictures of the car. Zinn patted Sydney's knee. "Let's go, kiddo. We're on!"

She got out the driver's side and the photographer greeted her at the front of the car, his camera mashed against his face as he snapped away and backed up at the same time. Sydney didn't feel as conspicuous and self-conscious as she'd expected. The whole thing was so ludicrous, it was almost fun.

Approaching Zinn, she tossed her head, letting the breeze carry her long hair back over her shoulder. He was grinning suavely as she stepped up onto the curb and into his arms. The crowd of patrons out front had been attracted by the commotion and had turned to watch. Sydney and Zinn stood still for a moment, facing the cameraman who was darting back and forth to get as many angles as he could.

Sydney heard Zinn's name on people's lips as the general excitement rose. Some young girl gave an excited squeal.

"Kiss her," the photographer prompted, orchestrating the scenario a bit.

Zinn complied, kissing Sydney on the temple. His hand was around her waist and he was pulling her against his body. They looked into each other's smiling eyes.

"It's a hell of a lot more fun in private," Zinn said under his breath.

"I see what you mean," Sydney responded, without breaking her smile.

A young woman with a recorder hanging from her shoulder and a microphone in her hand stepped forward. She was a brash blonde with a no-nonsense expression on her face. "This the girl?" she asked, without bothering with an introduction.

"Yes," Zinn replied. "Sydney Charles."

"With an *i* or a *y*?" the reporter demanded.

"*Y*," Sydney said.

The microphone moved before Zinn's mouth. "What's the story, Zinn?" the reporter questioned. "You two engaged, or what?"

"Sydney and I are very good friends."

The reporter rocked her head back and forth in a mocking fashion. "Et cetera, et cetera."

"Right. Et cetera, et cetera."

"So, if you're such a good friends, why did she send you to the hospital?"

"It was a misunderstanding," Zinn replied. "Passions run high when people care for each other." He gave Sydney's waist a firm squeeze.

"What did you hit him with, Sydney?"

She glanced at Zinn.

"Her fist," he said. "She's really very strong."

The reporter snapped some gum she was chewing. "You're sorry about it now, Sydney?"

"Oh, yes. I really love him. You can't imagine how terrible I felt when I saw what I'd done." Sydney knew she sounded like a bimbo, but that was the point. It was exactly what she wanted Barbara to think. Again, Zinn gave her a squeeze.

"What did he do to get you so pissed off that you'd clobber him?"

Sydney raised her brows haughtily. "I got jealous. I hate it when other women look at him."

Zinn groaned faintly in her ear. "You're in the wrong business, honey," he whispered.

"How old are you, Sydney?" the reporter asked.

"Twenty-five."

"What do you do?"

"Telecommunications," Zinn said, quickly answering for her.

The reporter glanced at him disbelievingly, but didn't comment. "You from L.A., Sydney?"

"At the moment, she's staying with me," Zinn responded.

"We're just inseparable," Sydney added.

"I'm taking her with me on location to San Francisco in a couple of days when the *For the Defense* crew heads north."

"But you're just friends, right?"

"For the moment."

Sydney held up her hand. "No rings yet."

"Anything more on the kidnapping you can tell us about, Zinn?" the reporter asked.

"We're confident the danger is over. We'd like to think this woman who's been harassing me has had her fill, and will leave us alone."

"You feel you're in any danger?" the reporter asked Sydney.

"Why should I be? I've never done anything to anybody."

The reporter rolled her eyes. She was such a smug, obnoxious creature, that Sydney would have loved to pop her one. But she could imagine the headline in the grocery-store tabloid, if she did: Zinn Garrett's Mystery Lover, Three Months Pregnant With Twins, Clobbers TV Reporter With Twelve-Carat Diamond Peace Offering From Actor.

Onlookers began crowding in to listen. Sydney heard a couple of young girls in back shouting, "It's Zinn Garrett!"

The fans crowded in then. Slips of paper were shoved Zinn's way, and he dutifully signed his name.

The reporter gave him a distressed look. "Come on, Zinn, give me something juicy."

"We're happier than ever," he replied. "The incident has brought us together. This girl just might be the love of my life." He signed a few more autographs, then begged leave to go inside. "I'm still a bit light-headed from my injury, so you'll have to excuse us."

They pushed on through the small crowd to the door where the hostess was waiting with a smile. Sydney was glad to get into the relative quiet and calm of the restaurant. Zinn gave his car keys to a young man who went outside to take care of the Jaguar.

"Is it like this every time you go somewhere for a hamburger?" Sydney asked as they made their way around the center bar.

"Only when I insist on coming in with trumpets blaring." He kept his arm around her waist as he guided her to their table.

"How do you stand it?"

"I usually don't go places with trumpets blaring. I'm doing this to accommodate you and your battle plan."

Sydney smiled. "What are you saying? That you hate the attention?"

"Hard as you may find it to believe, Syd, I consider it a price I have to pay. It's times like this I wish I'd stayed in law school."

They sat down at a rather quiet booth. A waitress in a white uniform and apron showed up at once to take their order. Zinn wanted a San Miguel beer and a hamburger. Sydney decided on mineral water and a salad.

The people sitting around them stared a lot. One little girl was brave enough to come over for an autograph. A couple of teenage girls followed. Zinn joked with them and signed their napkins, sending them off with a wink.

"Were you a heartthrob in high school, too?" Sydney asked.

"No, I was your classic nerd. I studied all the time, though I was on the swim team."

"Really?"

"Honest."

"I pictured you as the lead in all the school plays."

"I was in one or two. Mainly because a girl I had a crush on was in the drama club."

"Where was that?"

"Tucson, Arizona. My dad sold insurance. My mom taught grade school."

"You were just a regular guy, weren't you?" she teased.

Zinn grinned. "I still am, honey bun. The problem is, some people refuse to see me that way."

Suddenly serious, Sydney shook her head. "Sorry, but a guy living with all this adulation is not a regular guy. I don't care what you say."

"To them I'm not, maybe. But I know who I am. I also know how phony Grant Adams is. I'm not him any more than my dad was the insurance policy he sold. That was his work, this is mine. Dad's family and friends were what mattered to him. My family and friends are what matter to me."

Sydney didn't say anything for a minute. She was taking it all in. Then she asked, "Are your parents still living?"

"My mother is. She and Andrea are really close. I considered sending Andrea to Tucson for a while, but then it occurred to me Barbara might try to grab her there. I didn't want my mother to have to face that prospect."

Sydney listened with rapt attention. It was the first time she'd been with Zinn in public. The adulation he attracted as a TV star was in marked contrast to the down-to-earth guy who was talking to her. After a while, she realized she was sitting with her chin in her hand, as mesmerized by him as the people staring from around the room. The difference was, she was seeing a totally different man.

The waitress brought their food. Zinn signed another autograph for a lady visiting from Nebraska. They ate for a while in silence.

"How is your ex taking this business with Barbara?" Sydney asked. She'd wondered about his marriage, but hadn't found an easy way to broach the subject before.

"She was out of the country when the kidnapping attempt took place. I called her manager and explained the steps I was taking. Monica phoned once from Africa, as soon as she heard, to speak to Andrea. I talked to her for a few minutes to make sure she understood everything was all right. I calmed her down, and we haven't heard from her since."

"She has to be concerned."

"Oh, she is. Monica's decent enough. She loves Andrea, of course. But underneath it all, she's just glad she doesn't have to be the primary parent."

"Is that why you divorced?"

Zinn rubbed his chin, considering his answer. "I wouldn't say that, no. If you want to know the truth, I think it was because Monica took this town and herself a lot more seriously than I did. She was obsessed with attaining stardom, and it really galled her that I couldn't care less about that side of it, especially when my career took off and hers didn't. Our outlooks were so opposed, it ended up tearing us apart."

Sydney looked into his eyes and didn't doubt his sincerity.

Zinn took a long drink of beer, leaning back for a moment in his chair. "I'll tell you how Monica and I were different," he said. "You know the image of me you had when you arrived at my house?"

"Yeah."

"Well, that's the way Monica really is. And you know the person you are under that miniskirt facade you're wearing today? That's more like me. You're just putting on an act, Syd, because at the moment it's your job. That's the way it is for me, too."

"Our life-styles aren't at all the same, though."

"If there's a difference between us, Sydney, it's that you take yourself a hell of a lot more seriously than I do."

"What do you mean by that?"

"I still haven't seen you lighten up. Like I said before, you always seem to be on duty."

Sydney took a last bite of salad and pushed her plate away. "When you go to work, you put on your Grant Adams face. When I go to work, I put on my gun."

"No," he said, shaking his head. "I don't think you understand what I mean."

The man at the next table tapped Zinn on the shoulder and asked if he could have an autograph for his teenage daughter who was at home, ill with a kidney disease. The wife said that his show was the girl's favorite TV program. Zinn told the couple if they would give him an address he'd have an autographed photo sent to their daughter. This pleased them immensely, and the man jotted down an address.

Afterward, Zinn signaled the waitress for the check and looked at Sydney. "I don't know about you, but I've had enough Grant Adams for today. I'm ready to go home and be me."

Sydney was ready to leave, too. But she wasn't a hundred-percent sure which Zinn Garrett she'd be going back with—the heartthrob of millions of women, or the man she had come to regard as an individual with an outlook not so very different from her own.

6

Zinn was surprisingly taciturn during the trip back to Pacific Palisades. Sydney, who drove again, didn't feel a lot like talking, either. She was still trying to sort out her emotions. Zinn had her thoroughly confused. But she reminded herself that one thing was clear—she had a job to do.

"Do you think that song and dance we went through will do any good?" she asked after a long silence.

"I suspect it will generate the publicity we want. After that, I guess it's up to Barbara."

"And who knows what she'll do? Dealing with a mentally unbalanced criminal is probably the most difficult aspect of law enforcement. Rational principles don't apply." She glanced at him and found him watching her again. For some reason, though, there seemed to be a touch of sadness in his eyes. "What's the matter, Zinn?"

"I don't know. I'm a little tired, maybe."

"Is that really it?"

"I guess I was also thinking about you—how incongruous the way you look right now is with who you really are."

As she drove, she glanced down at herself. "This miniskirt is a costume."

"Yes, I know."

"You, of all people, should be able to relate to that."

"Right."

They lapsed into silence again. Sydney fought off disquieting thoughts of Zinn by trying to keep her mind on the case. The problem Barbara posed was not an easy one. All they could do was provide the opportunity for her to act, and to be ready for her when she did. "Tell me about San Francisco," she said. "What will the routine be like?"

He outlined the normal activities of a location shoot. The work was almost entirely outdoors. The production crew had scheduled a number of night and day location shoots at various places in the city. He described the setup, the security, a typical daily schedule.

"If Barbara has any understanding of the business," Sydney said, "she'll realize this trip is an ideal opportunity for her."

"I'd much prefer the police pick her up first," Zinn replied. "I don't like the brunt of this falling on you."

Sydney wasn't going to argue with him. He was, after all, only demonstrating his concern. But what surprised her most was his growing emotion about the subject.

They arrived home to find everything in order. Jack Dowd was watching a baseball game on TV. Yolanda and Andrea were baking cookies in the kitchen. Dowd took off right away, saying he'd make himself available when they needed him. Zinn said he was going to his den to study lines. When Andrea begged to go for a swim, Zinn asked Sydney if she'd supervise. Then he went off with a pile of scripts under his arm.

Sydney and Andrea got into their suits and went out to the pool. They were there for a couple of hours, including some time in lounge chairs in the sun. Once, while they were in the pool, Zinn came out and watched them with a glass of iced tea in his hand. Then, without a word, he went back to his work.

That night he had to attend a dinner meeting with the show's producers. Before he left, he knocked on Sydney's door to talk with her about his schedule. She had showered and washed her hair and was in her robe, sitting up in bed. Her hair was still wet. Zinn stayed near the door as they talked.

"I don't know what time I'll be getting home," he said, "but I can tell you this—I'm definitely coming in the front door."

She laughed and Zinn smiled back at her. He looked especially handsome in a double-breasted navy blazer and pale lavender silk shirt and tie. Sydney knew she was becoming more susceptible to his appeal all the time, and there was only one way to guard against it— she had to stick to business.

"I had a call from Manny Ibáñez, the lighting contractor, a while ago," she told him. "He had some recommendations and an estimate."

"If it seems reasonable, have him do the work. I trust your judgment."

Again she was aware of something different in his attitude and demeanor. But she couldn't put her finger on it. Zinn stayed at the door, almost as though he were shy. "Well," she said, "have a good time this evening."

"I'd invite you to come along, but there's no publicity value in it, and these meetings can be terribly tedious."

"It's much more important that I stay with Andrea. Anyway, you can't afford having both Jack and me on the payroll. As it is, I feel badly that you have to pay him to stay here while I go with you to San Francisco, especially since it was my idea."

"Don't be silly. The money's not a factor. You know how I feel about Andrea's security."

She nodded, feeling as tentative as he appeared to be.

"There's something else, Syd," he said, shifting his weight from one foot to the other, almost like a nervous teenager. "Michael Douglas's new film is premiering here in L.A. next Saturday. And that definitely is a publicity event—an opportunity for us to be seen together. I think you should plan on going with me."

"That's after we get back from San Francisco. We might not need any more publicity by then."

"You may be right. But you could go with me anyway. I don't have another date and you seem to be able to hack the Hollywood scene for a few hours at a time. We can chuckle out of the corners of our mouths together."

For some reason, the notion of going to a premiere with Zinn was very appealing. But Sydney questioned whether it was a good idea. Then she rationalized that it was entirely possible that Barbara would still be at large. And duty dictated that she do whatever was needed to draw the woman out. "Okay," she agreed. "I'll go with you."

Zinn smiled, looking truly happy for the first time during the conversation. "I've got to run," he said. "Stay safe."

"You, too. If you notice anybody following you, head for a police station."

He gave a thumbs-up and left the room.

WHEN SYDNEY GOT UP the next morning, Zinn had already gone to the studio. Yolanda gave her an envelope that he'd left for her. Inside, along with a credit card, was a note.

Syd,
We leave for S.F. tomorrow afternoon at three. Pack for three days. If you need clothes, use the

credit card. Call Jack and have him stay with Yolanda and Andrea. Yolanda will order a limo. While you're shopping, get yourself a gown for the premiere on Saturday evening. Something sexy is de rigueur—you gotta look the part, in case Barbara is still on the loose.

By the way, we made *Entertainment Tonight* last night. They got hold of the picture of us together at the Hard Rock. Judy was pleased. I'll try and get a tape, if you're interested.

Zinn

Zinn seemed to appreciate the fact that she had neither the wardrobe nor the money to socialize Hollywood-style, and she was grateful for the way he had solved her problem. He was not without sensitivity. She had noticed that in the way he dealt with his fans, as well.

While a shopping spree seemed like an exciting prospect, there were problems. Sydney only had one day to get ready for San Francisco, and she had no desire to embarrass Zinn by the way she was dressed. Picking out a couple of outfits wouldn't be hard, but the dress for the premiere really had her concerned. She had never shopped for that kind of thing before and hadn't the slightest idea what would be appropriate.

Having decided her mother was the best free source she could muster, Sydney invited her along on the shopping trip. After making arrangements for Jack Dowd to come over, she asked Yolanda to order the limo. An hour later she was on her way to Glendale.

When she arrived at her mother's house, Lee greeted her at the door, decked out in her finest. "Sydney, darling, I've just been dying to know what's going on! After you called, Gladys Waitley telephoned. She said you and Zinn were mentioned last night on *Entertainment Tonight*. I missed it. What's happened?"

"For starters, Mother, I'm not in the movie business, so don't get your heart all aflutter. That was just something the publicity people arranged to divert attention from Zinn's daughter. I'm sort of playing an undercover role, and the purpose of today's trip is to buy my costumes." She took Lee by the arm and led her out to the limo, where the driver was holding the door for them.

Lee smiled at the man. "We'll be going to Westwood."

"Yes, ma'am."

She peered into the plush interior of the automobile, then turned to her daughter. "Sydney, I don't know what's going on, but I couldn't be more thrilled."

"Believe me, Mother, it's not as thrilling as you make it out to be." They climbed into the limo. "It's part of the job, that's all."

"How glorious! Where are you going, and when?"

"The premiere of Michael Douglas's new film, and it's not until Saturday. But the dress has to be purchased today. For the next couple of days I'm going to be in San Francisco with Zinn, on location."

Lee gasped with sheer delight.

"Don't make anything out of that, either, Mother."

"Sydney..."

"It's business. Nothing more."

The chauffeur started the car and they pulled away.

"Truly, darling?" Lee prodded. "Isn't a tiny part of you absolutely thrilled by this? For years I've felt that all you needed was to experience it firsthand, especially on the arm of a man you cared for. Who knows where it might lead? Opportunities you hadn't even dreamed of could come along. Surely Zinn's seen how lovely you are. You've got that indescribable quality. All you have to do is let go." Lee took her hand. "This is your chance, darling! Seize the day!"

Sydney looked into her mother's eyes and was overcome by feelings of sadness. The poor thing was so excited she was shaking. The hope Lee had clung to for years seemed to have turned into a genuine opportunity, and how was Sydney going to convince her that wasn't what it was at all?

"Mother, I know you say these things out of love, but you really don't understand. That is not what my relationship with Zinn is all about."

Lee looked skeptical. "You mean he didn't even hint that you ought to be in pictures?"

Sydney shook her head. "I'm afraid not."

"Well, tell me this. Does he at least like you?"

"I suppose so. It's been rough at times, but I'd say we have a decent working relationship. It's strictly business, though." Sydney felt disingenuous, but how was she going to admit that some sort of connection had formed between them, without giving her mother false hope? As it was, the poor woman had no sense of proportion.

Lee looked disappointed.

"Mom, I told you I was serious about my career."

Lee disregarded the remark. "He must have flirted. I don't see how he couldn't have."

Sydney glanced out the window to avoid her mother's eyes.

"He kissed you, didn't he?"

Sydney gave her a frightful glare. Lee slapped her knee with glee. "I knew it! I knew it! How could he not adore the most beautiful girl in Hollywood!"

It was easier for Sydney not to reply. Her dreams were about all Lee had left. It seemed preferable to let her have them. Sydney's only obligation was to be honest—and not create any false hope. In a matter of days the job could be over and Zinn Garrett would be out of her life.

"Now dear," her mother said, after they'd driven in silence for a few minutes, "I suppose you want to hear my plan for your gown."

"Sure. I've put you in charge."

"I've done some calling around town. You remember me talking about Nola Jiménez, don't you?"

"No, not really."

"Well, she's just plain Nola now. When I knew her she worked as a seamstress for Edith Head. We used to have lunch together when things were slow at the studio, which was all too often for me. Anyway, she's a designer now, does custom work. In the last few years she's caught on and a number of the stars use her. They say her shop's lovely."

"We're going to a custom designer?" She could see that her mother was going whole hog on this one.

"You *are* going to a premiere, aren't you? With a star? You *will* be seen."

"Moth-er, it's not that big a deal."

"What's our budget?"

She shrugged. "Zinn didn't say."

Lee thought. "I suppose Nola will give us something she's already done for, say, three or four thousand. Lord knows, there's not time to design something from scratch. Would Zinn spring for that?"

"I suppose so, if that's the going rate. But I don't want to take advantage of the situation and be extravagant."

"Sydney, darling, there's only looking sensational or being a flop."

"Four thousand is as sensational as I'm willing to look."

"All right. We'll make do. I told Nola on the phone you were an eight."

"I am, mostly."

"She said she has three or four possibles, including a gorgeous dress a very well-known client turned down because of unpleasant associations with another gown and a man."

Sydney laughed. "Considering I was one step from shopping at the Goodwill store last week, I don't suppose I can be choosy."

"Panache, darling. Think panache. Nola is a friend, but we want her to think you're worthy of one of her gowns. And, of course, her name must be mentioned if anyone asks about the designer."

"Of course."

Lee noticed Sydney looking out the back window of the limousine. "Darling, why do you keep turning around? The driver's not speeding."

"I know."

"Is something bothering you?"

"I'm observant by nature, Mother. It's an occupational characteristic."

"Well, I wish you'd forget the gumshoe business for a day or two. You're riding the crest of a very important wave. And you *are* off duty, aren't you?"

"I wish I were."

Lee looked puzzled, but she didn't seem to think it worth getting a clarification. "Nola said one of the gowns was a soft ivory. Depending on the design, it might look a little too bridal. On the other hand, with your coloring, it might be perfect."

Nodding, Sydney leaned back. But she clutched her purse close to her side. Dreams were wonderful, but life also had its share of nightmares.

WHEN SYDNEY GOT HOME, Yolanda greeted her at the door. Andrea hadn't wanted to take a nap, so she was watching television. Zinn was studying a script and Jack Dowd had already left. Sydney had an armload of dresses from exclusive stores to take along to San Francisco. The housekeeper helped her carry them to her room.

"You got a dress for the big party?" Yolanda asked.

"I bought one, but I don't pick it up until Saturday. They had to do some alterations."

"I bet it is beautiful, *señorita*."

Sydney had to smile. The dress was lovely. They'd settled on the ivory one, and though it did have a hint of bride about it, she'd looked terrific in it.

Yolanda smiled at Sydney. "You want to rest before dinner. Maybe you a little tired, no?"

Sydney dropped onto the bed. "I'm exhausted, but to be honest, what I need is some real exercise."

"Exercise? You crazy?"

"No, I need to run, give my lungs and heart a workout. I wouldn't mind a little time in a weight room, too, but that's a little tougher, considering we don't have one here."

The housekeeper shook her head. "Girls are not the same these days. I must be old, *señorita*. I don't understand it."

"Women have muscles, the same as men. We used to pretend we didn't, that's all."

Yolanda shook her head again and headed for the door. "For me, I rather see you in a pretty dress. But I'm only the housekeeper. What do I know, anyway?"

Sydney smiled as Yolanda left, and went to get her pale blue jogging suit from her drawer. Running in the hills for a while would be a good way to get a quick workout.

As she dressed, she thought about her mother. Lee had prattled on during the entire shopping spree, refusing to let go of her dreams. Sydney loved her mother's spirited determination to see her succeed, but she had trouble with the fact that Lee defined success by the dreams that she herself hadn't realized. The one consolation was that today Lee had seemed happier than she'd been in years.

At Nola's, her mother had put on a stellar performance. One would have thought she was the dowager queen of Hollywood, rather than one of its abused castoffs. But Sydney was glad to have given her a thrill. Dreamers needed a touch of reinforcement from time to time to keep them going. Misplaced hope, perhaps, was better than none at all.

But as much as she worried about her mother, Sydney was even more concerned about Zinn Garrett. When she first met him, she was sure she had the situation pegged. He was an actor and that pretty much told the tale. Even the attraction she felt for him didn't take her too much by surprise; her father had been a pretty compelling individual, too—not only to her mother, but to her.

But even if Zinn was a different kind of man than her father, he still lived in a phony world where truth and make-believe were often indistinguishable. He might laugh at Hollywood now and then, but he didn't eschew the life-style. On the other hand, Sydney knew in her heart that it wasn't Hollywood per se that she'd been bitter about over the years; it was the way her father had used his work to shield himself from her and her mother. Zinn hadn't done that with Andrea. To the contrary, Sydney had no doubt that if it came down to choosing between his daughter and his career, he'd take Andrea.

So, where did that leave her, besides confused? Sydney wished she didn't feel so drawn to him. It would be a lot easier. She knew darned well that if he hadn't been an actor, and if she hadn't been working for him, she would have wanted a lot more than just a kiss. But under the circumstances, getting involved simply wasn't practical.

Having finished tying her sneakers, Sydney bounced up, determined to work off a little of the tension she'd felt building. The other members of the household were out of sight as she left. She paused in the front yard to do some stretching, then slowly jogged down to the gate, punched the security code into the panel to let herself out. Once on the street, she took off at a brisk pace down the hill.

Sydney had only gone fifty or sixty yards when she heard the roar of the engine behind her and knew instinctively that the car was going to run her down! With only the briefest glance back, she saw the sedan— driven by a redhead—bearing down on her. She dove into the shrubs bordering the street, barely evading the fender, which nicked her foot as she sailed through the air and landed hard on her right hip and shoulder.

Her heart pumping adrenaline, Sydney clambered out of the bushes as the car continued down the street at top speed. It was too far away to get the full license number, but she caught a glimpse of the first three letters. The sedan disappeared while Sydney stood staring, her chest heaving.

After a moment, she limped over to a nearby tree and leaned against it, rubbing her hip. The climactic moment had come and she hadn't been ready for it. Barbara had made an attempt, and all Sydney could say about it was that she had survived.

Brushing off a few leaves, she took stock of herself. Her shoulder and hip would be bruised, but she was sure there was no serious damage. Her heel hurt a bit where the fender had nicked it—she flexed her ankle, deciding it was probably a bone bruise. Annoyed and angry with herself, Sydney limped back to the house to give Marvin Kaslow a call. Now there was another piece to add to the puzzle.

SYDNEY HAD GOTTEN HOLD OF Kaslow without alerting Zinn or Yolanda about what had happened. She reasoned there was no need to get everybody in a tizzy. Later she could advise Zinn, so that he would know that the danger remained real and immediate.

After taking off her shoe to check her heel, Sydney went down to the gate to wait for the detective. Marvin Kaslow, a New York transplant with a distinctive accent and a sour expression, arrived within twenty minutes.

"I was on my way home when your call came in," he said, "but I figured, what the hell, I don't have anything better to do than work a couple more hours."

"Sorry I couldn't have scheduled it at a more convenient time," Sydney replied.

Kaslow's rumpled hair and styleless suit telegraphed he was a cop, since cops as a group weren't the sharpest dressers. Sydney explained what had happened.

"But ya didn't get a good look at her?" he said, chewing on a toothpick.

"No. Just an impression of red hair."

"You're sure?"

"I only had a glimpse, Marvin."

"Well, we'll see where the plate leads. This might be the break we've been looking for."

"At least it appears my strategy is paying off."

"What strategy?" Kaslow asked.

Sydney explained her plan to transfer Barbara's hostility from Andrea to her. She mentioned the publicity campaign and told him about the trip to San Francisco.

Kaslow nodded, impressed. "You've got more balls than I'd have thought, kid. Let's just hope your plan doesn't get you killed." He looked at his watch. "Mind if I use the phone? I ought to get this stuff on the license plate to the Department of Motor Vehicles computers."

"Sure." Sydney wasn't eager to have Kaslow doing his police work in the house, but she couldn't shield the family from everything.

As they entered in the front door, Zinn was walking through the hallway.

"Detective Kaslow," he said, looking startled. "What brings you up here?"

"An assault is an assault, even if the victim is a P.I. The department don't take things like this lightly."

Zinn looked confused. "What assault?"

"Your girl, Barbara, tried to run Miss Charles down." Kaslow looked at Sydney. "Didn't you tell him?"

Zinn came toward them. "Barbara was here? When was this?"

"Half an hour ago," she replied. "It happened out front, when I went jogging. No big deal, Zinn. Nothing to get excited about."

"Nothing to get excited about? Somebody tries to run you down and you say it's nothing to get excited about?" He was practically shouting by the time he'd finished.

Sydney looked into his eyes. He appeared upset. Maybe even a little angry. "This is exactly what we hoped for," she said calmly. "Unfortunately, though, I wasn't in a position to nab her."

Zinn's mouth dropped open in disbelief.

"Well, listen, kids," Kaslow said. "While you hash this out I'm going to make a few calls. I'll use the phone in the kitchen, okay?"

"Sure." They pointed him in the right direction, then Zinn took her face in his hands, looking at her closely. "Sydney, were you hurt?"

She shook her head. "No, not really. The fender grazed my heel and I landed kind of hard in the bushes, but I'm all right."

"Lord . . ." Zinn suddenly took her in his arms as though she were a child who'd been snatched from danger in the nick of time. The gesture amused her at first, but then she noticed the delicious aroma of his cologne, and she became aware of the pressure of his body against hers.

Then Zinn stepped back, taking her by the shoulders.

"I want to see where you were hurt."

"Zinn, it's nothing."

"Come on. I want to look at that foot." He took her by the hand and led her into the front room, where he made her sit down on one of the big white sofas. On his knees, he unlaced her running shoe, removing it gingerly. Then he took off her sock.

When he ran his fingers over her foot, tenderly, almost lovingly, Sydney shivered. His gentle affection got to her. Carefully he felt her heel, looking up into her eyes for signs of pain.

"Hurt?"

She smiled. "No. If anything, it tickles." That wasn't quite true, but she certainly wasn't going to admit his touch was arousing her.

Suddenly Zinn pressed a bit more firmly, causing a twinge of pain. She flinched.

"Aha!" he exclaimed.

Sydney gave him a look. "Well, what do you expect?"

"I'm confirming the diagnosis."

She pulled her foot away and put her sock back on. "So, you think you're a podiatrist now?"

"I want you to have it treated."

"Don't be silly. I've had worse bone bruises from running on rocks."

Kaslow appeared at the door. "Good chance the car was a rental," he said. "We ran it through the computer. It's the best fit of all the possibles."

"Barbara's a bit more wily than your everyday nut case," Sydney observed.

"Yeah, looks that way."

"Will you let me know if you get a line on her?"

"Sure. You'll be the first to know." Kaslow gestured toward the front door with his thumb. "I'll be taking off. Someone else can take a formal statement from you tomorrow, Syd, if you don't mind."

"Sure, but make it early. We're going to San Francisco in the afternoon."

Kaslow grinned. "You've got a real firecracker there, Mr. Garrett." Waving at them both, the detective left.

Zinn looked at her, the corner of his mouth twitching. "Yep, a real firecracker."

"Oh, shut up!" Sydney said.

She got up, but Zinn pulled her back down on the sofa. Before she knew it, his body was half over her. He had her jaw in his hand, his mouth was hovering just inches from hers.

Zinn wanted badly to taste her lips. And so he kissed her, gently pressing his mouth to hers. He heard her give a little moan of protest, but it wasn't determined or angry. Her body went slack, and she put her hand behind his neck, digging her fingers into his hair as she kissed him back.

She came alive in his arms and his desire deepened. This was what he'd been wanting for days. He wasn't sure what it was that had set him off. Maybe it was holding her slender foot in his hand. Maybe it was just knowing she'd been hurt. Whatever it was, his concern, his compassion and his desire all flared at once.

When his lips finally broke from hers, he kissed the corner of her mouth. Sydney slowly opened her eyes and smiled at him. "I thought you were supposed to kiss the spot of the injury to make it better," she teased.

He grinned at her. "That can be arranged. But now may not be the best time." He eased himself off her and stood. "I really am serious about you seeing a doctor, Syd. You might be more seriously hurt than you think. There could be a hairline fracture . . . anything."

Sydney shook her head and got up. As she rose she felt a twinge in her hip, and she knew she'd be stiff the next day. "I really am fine. But maybe I will rest for a while before dinner, if you don't mind."

He glanced down at his thin gold watch. "Sure. Take as long as you want. Yolanda is going to a movie with her sister tonight, so we might as well suit ourselves. I'll have her feed Andrea and put her to bed before she leaves, though. She missed her nap today, so she'll be pretty tired. Then you and I can eat whenever we get hungry."

"Sounds good." Sydney headed down the hall. Zinn watched her, noticing that she favored the bruised foot. As she disappeared into her room and he heard the door shut, he thought again about their kiss. This time she hadn't rebuffed him. She had responded as though she wanted him every bit as much as he wanted her. Most important, she hadn't been defensive afterward. Maybe he was making progress with her, after all. Maybe he had gotten through to her that afternoon and she was beginning to see him as a man, not just an actor.

SYDNEY STRETCHED OUT on her bed and tried to relax. But when she closed her eyes, she immediately recalled Zinn's kiss. She could almost smell his cologne, feel the warmth of his breath on her cheek. She sat up abruptly, trying to erase the image from her mind, but it was no use. Ever since that afternoon at the Hard Rock, she had seen Zinn in a new light.

She'd known from the first that she was attracted to him, but that hadn't seemed to matter so long as she focused on her job. But, as vexing as Barbara was proving to be, Sydney's interest in the woman paled aside her interest in Zinn. For the first time in her life, a man seemed more compelling than a case.

She gave up trying to rest and sat up to examine her foot. When she pulled off her sock she could see that a dark bruise was starting to form. She got up and headed for the bathroom, where she peeled off her jogging suit. Sure enough, her right shoulder and hip were starting to color, too. She rotated her shoulder, testing the extent of the tenderness in her gun arm. Fortunately it wasn't too bad. Her hip was another story. It was quite sore and seemed to have taken the worst of it.

She decided to take a hot shower before dinner, and save a longer soak in the tub for just before going to bed.

A minute later, after she had twisted her hair up on top of her head, Sydney stepped under the sensuous spray. As the warm water ran over her skin, she thought again of Zinn, and the feel of his body over hers as he'd kissed her.

Knowing that fantasies wouldn't get her anywhere, she soaped herself quickly and lowered the temperature of the water. That wouldn't do much to ease the soreness, but she rationalized that it might put an end to her thoughts of Zinn.

After she dried off, Sydney slipped into her terry robe and returned to her bed. Her hip was throbbing a little. Zinn was on her mind, as well. It hadn't taken much for him to bedevil her—a kiss, and that was it.

She did manage to doze off, slipping into one of those dreamy states between sleep and wakefulness. Once, in the back of her consciousness, she thought she heard Andrea's voice out in the hall, but the sound faded and she drifted into a deeper sleep.

Sometime later a knock on the bedroom door awakened her. Sydney sat up in bed, looking at the clock. It was after eight-thirty. "Yes?"

"It's me," Zinn said through the door. "Can I come in?"

"I'm not dressed."

"That sounds good."

A smile played at the corner of her mouth. "That's all a matter of point of view."

"How are you feeling?"

"Fine."

"How about a few minutes in the spa to relax those stiff bones and sore muscles before we eat?"

Sydney rolled the idea over in her mind. The prospect of the soothing warm water loosening her muscles was appealing. "All right. I'll get on my suit."

"I'll turn on the spa and be back in a few minutes."

She got up, feeling suddenly energized. Digging her bikini out of the drawer, she headed off for the bathroom to change.

After she'd slipped on her black-and-white swimsuit, Sydney looked at herself in the mirror. As she turned from one side to the other to examine her body, she knew there was no way that Zinn wouldn't notice the enormous bruise on her thigh. Her shoulder didn't look too bad, though. She shrugged, deciding that since there wasn't much she could do about it, there was no point in worrying.

She went back into the bedroom, and was taking a shirt out of her drawer to wear as a cover-up, when Zinn knocked again. Holding the garment in front of her chest, she called for him to enter.

He opened the door and she saw at once that he had on the same black trunks as before. He hadn't bothered with a shirt, and her gaze was drawn at once to his chest. Zinn looked absolutely fabulous. For some reason, she hadn't focused on that aspect when she'd agreed to get into the spa with him. She'd simply told herself that the water would be therapeutic for her hip. Ha! So much for being in touch with her feelings, she thought.

"Are you ready?" he asked.

"Almost." She unconsciously wet her lips. "Has Yolanda left?"

"Yes. And I put Andrea to bed. She fell asleep right away. We'll be alone."

Sydney looked at him, knowing what he meant, and unable to protest. She started to slip the shirt on, but winced when she pulled her arm back to slip it into the armhole. Zinn was at her side at once.

"Let me see that." He gently moved the shirt aside and looked at her shoulder.

As his fingers grazed her skin, she shivered. "It's bruised a little, but it isn't bad. I'm sure the spa will fix me up."

He leaned over and lightly kissed the top of her shoulder. "That ought to make it better," he said.

Sydney wanted to reply, but she couldn't. She was holding her breath. Her skin felt alive where his lips had touched her. She looked into Zinn's eyes, and that same feeling returned as when he had kissed her earlier. Only this time they weren't in the living room. And they were alone.

"Zinn . . ."

He put his arm around her good shoulder and pressed his face into the soft flesh of her neck. She felt his breath on her skin.

"Zinn . . ."

His other arm slipped around her waist and he kissed her ear.

She said, "I really don't think . . ."

But he paid no attention, kissing her more earnestly, arousing her. His lips slid to her mouth and he nibbled at the fullness of her lower lip.

"Oh, Lord . . . Zinn, I . . ."

His mouth covered hers and he kissed her tenderly at first. When the pressure mounted, she put her arms around his neck. Then they walked over to the bed together. He eased her gently down. A moment later he was on top of her, kissing her passionately.

Without even realizing what she was doing, Sydney slid her hand across his chest. The warmth of his skin felt electric. She burrowed her fingers in the furry mat as he kissed her, and she knew that this was what she had longed for. She had wanted to run her hands over his chest ever since she'd first seen him at the pool.

Zinn responded by untying the top of her suit and pushing the fabric aside. Then slowly, ever so slowly, he lowered his face to her breast. When his tongue began painting moist circles around her nub, Sydney moaned. When both nipples were wet he pulled his head away and gently blew over them. She shivered and felt a hot rush of liquid between her legs.

He began sucking her breast then, pulling gently with his teeth and teasing her nipple with his tongue. Just when she thought she couldn't take any more pleasure, she felt his fingers trail up her thigh to the edge of her bikini bottom. Then he pushed the fabric aside and touched her. Sydney moaned, parting her legs to him, and Zinn started to play with her moist curls, delicately probing with his finger.

Sydney wanted to pleasure him as he was pleasuring her, so she lowered her hand to massage him through the fabric of his swim trunks. She closed her eyes and relished the sensation. It had been a long time since she'd been with anyone, and yet she wasn't afraid. She didn't feel shy or nervous; she only felt the hard edge of desire. She knew she wanted Zinn Garrett, and she wanted him now.

Opening her eyes, Sydney pulled away from him a bit. Then she reached down to strip off the rest of her swimsuit.

Zinn kissed her cheek, then her nose. "Are you protected?" he asked.

She shook her head. "I . . . didn't think—"

"I'll take care of it." He got off the bed and headed for the door. Sydney lay back on the bed and waited for him to return. The desire she felt was so great, it was like a raw, physical pain. Never had she wanted a man so much.

In a moment she heard the door open again. Zinn was back. He quickly stripped off his trunks and joined her on the bed. Her hand went to him at once. He was fully aroused, and she began running her fingers up and down his penis.

Again Zinn toyed with her curls, and trailed his fingers over the insides of her thighs. He seemed to know instinctively how to heighten her desire. And when she didn't think she could stand the teasing another minute, he touched her center and slipped his finger inside.

Sydney opened her legs wider and arched as he began rubbing her. Within minutes she knew it wasn't enough. She wanted more of him.

"Please, Zinn. Let's not wait any longer."

He moved over her, then. As she looked into his eyes she felt the tip of him touch her. She reached up and pulled his mouth down on her lips as he plunged into her. She gasped, but with delight. For several seconds he didn't move. Sydney knew he was giving her a chance to get used to the feel of him, but she couldn't keep from thrusting.

Zinn, too, must have tired of the teasing, because he began making love to her in earnest. He drove into her, rhythmically giving pleasure, then denying her. Sydney clutched the bedspread in her fists. Then she wrapped her legs around him, hoping to keep him inside her, yet knowing that the denial was an important part of the pleasure.

He continued to thrust until neither of them could hold back any longer. Sydney cried out his name, and almost at the same time she felt him stiffen and heave against her forcefully several times. Her cries of release overrode the urgent sound of his breathing, as wave after wave of exquisite sensation rippled from her core.

When he was spent, Zinn collapsed onto her and for a moment, neither of them moved. Then he rolled to his side so that she could breathe more easily.

Sydney looked into his eyes as she felt the cool air hit her chest. She wanted to tell him how wonderful she felt, but she couldn't find the words.

Zinn reached over and touched her lower lip. "You were fantastic, Sydney. I can't even begin to tell you how special you are to me."

She felt a tear form, and she lifted a hand to wipe it off, but Zinn must have noticed it, too, because he brushed it away with the backs of his fingers.

He looked concerned. "I didn't hurt you, did I?"

She shook her head.

He looked down to where her hand was resting on her hip, and moved it aside. Seeing the bruise, he gingerly touched her skin. "You didn't tell me about this."

"I didn't want to. Anyway, it's not bad."

"Not bad?" He looked into her eyes. "What else haven't you told me about?"

"Nothing else. Honest."

He took her chin in his hand. "What do you think you are, Syd, a marine or something?"

"No. I'm a five-hundred-dollar-a-day P.I. And I'm not paid to complain."

He brushed a strand of hair off her cheek. "Right now you're a beautiful girl with a nasty bruise. I'm going to get an ice pack and take care of that." He kissed her lip. "Promise you won't go away?"

"All right," she said, unable to hold back a smile. "I promise."

7

ZINN LOOKED IN ON ANDREA on his way to the kitchen. She was sleeping peacefully. He checked his watch, and knew that it would be some time before Yolanda returned home.

Opening the refrigerator, he spied some leftovers that could be reheated but not a lot of prepared foods, because Yolanda did most of her cooking from scratch. He wondered if Sydney might have some ideas about what they should eat.

Zinn sat at the kitchen table to wait for her. Between the sex, the spa and a hot shower, he felt wonderfully relaxed and mellow. Sydney Charles had thoroughly captivated him—and more than that, he was falling in love with her. It had only been a few days and they'd been intimate just this once, but his feelings already went far beyond simple physical attraction.

But, wonderful as he felt, a lot had to be clarified before their relationship could progress. Zinn knew he was fully capable of falling in love with someone like Sydney, but he was mature enough to know that his feelings were only a beginning. Monica had once set him on his heels, and look where that had ended.

After his divorce, Zinn had talked to his mother about the failure of his marriage. She'd told him that the ability to identify with your partner and commit selflessly to them was as much, or even more important, than romantic love. It had sounded pie-in-the-sky at the time, but over the years he'd come to understand the wisdom of those words. It remained to be seen just how well he and Sydney fit in that respect.

The other thing that concerned him was Barbara's broadening campaign to harm everyone that he held near and dear. The woman was a monster, and he could no longer accept the fact that Sydney was at risk of being seriously hurt by her.

"What, dinner's not ready yet?" Sydney was leaning against the doorframe, her arms folded over a navy blue terry robe. She was barefoot, her damp hair was combed out and hanging down her back.

Zinn, himself in a forest-green sweatsuit, got up as she walked to the table. He took her in his arms and kissed her. "I was waiting for the expert."

"Expert what, Zinn?"

"You do cook, don't you?"

Sydney shook her head. "Cereal for breakfast, peanut-butter-and-jelly sandwiches, hot dogs and soup for lunch, frozen dinners for supper. I also make Jell-O dessert, instant pudding, microwave cakes and frozen pies."

"My God . . . Now you tell me!"

She smiled at him, almost triumphantly. "If such things matter, you should have asked me before."

Zinn conjured up the most disillusioned expression he could muster.

"What about you?" she asked. "A lot of men cook, these days."

"If you thought that's what you were getting in me, you're going to be sorely disappointed."

Her eyes rounded as though she was horrified. "You don't cook, either?"

Zinn shook his head. "Yolanda was hired because she's as good in the kitchen as she is with children."

Sydney stroked her chin. "We've got a problem. Neither of us would make a very good wife."

He took her by the hand and led her to the refrigerator. He opened the door and stood gazing at the contents, his arm around her shoulders. "There *are* leftovers. You can handle heating some up, can't you?"

"If you've got a microwave, I can. But you'll have to set the table. Like everyone else, I've got my limits."

He bussed her on the cheek. "Sydney, my dear, our future together looks bleak, and it hasn't yet begun."

"My mother warned me men value cooking-and-cleaning skills. I should have listened to her."

The telephone rang just then, and Zinn answered it. It was Marvin Kaslow. He asked for Sydney.

"Syd," Zinn said, holding out the receiver. "It's for you."

While Sydney spoke on the phone, Zinn picked out a likely assortment of leftovers and arranged them on the counter. When he saw that the conversation would last a while, he began heating them in the microwave. It was hard for him to tell what was being said, and it was a long conversation. Sydney didn't get off the phone until he had practically everything warmed up.

She came over to the counter and helped him finish up and get the table ready. At first she didn't say anything about the phone call.

"So, what did Kaslow have to say?" he asked.

"They were able to get quite a bit on Barbara. But they haven't been able to pick her up."

"What sorts of things did they learn?"

Sydney filled a couple of glasses with ice water and carried them to the table. Zinn had dished the food onto the plates and brought them over, as well. They sat down and he looked at her, waiting for an answer.

"The cops are pretty sure the car Barbara used came from a Beverly Hills rental agency. From the information they got, they believe they've identified her."

Zinn felt a surge of joy. "They have? Who is she?"

"Kaslow said the name is Barbara Walsh. They're only beginning to trace her background, but there is a history of mental illness. They believe she worked in Hollywood at one time, and—this is the interesting part—she's from San Francisco originally." Their eyes met briefly, then Sydney picked up her fork. *"Bon appétit,"* she said.

"San Francisco?" He was a bit stunned by the news. She nodded as she chewed.

"But that means there's a good chance she will follow us there," Zinn said. "I mean, she'll know her way around town."

Sydney nodded again. "Yeah, but that's what we want."

Zinn looked down at his food. Moments earlier he'd been hungry, but suddenly he'd lost his appetite. Sydney, it seemed, was not similarly afflicted.

For a moment or two he watched her. She glanced up at him, her wonderful blue eyes questioning what must have been a dismayed expression on his face.

"Do you really think this San Francisco trip is such a good idea?" he asked.

She laughed. "Zinn, we're closing in on her. She probably senses it, and is getting ready to act. Kaslow also told me that this evening she called the station that carries *Entertainment Tonight* and made a death threat against me."

"Oh, great."

"It's not exactly a surprise," Sydney replied. "She's already tried once. But the more overeager and careless she is, the better. From our standpoint, this might be the perfect time for the kill."

"Don't you mean the perfect time to get killed?"

She gave him a look.

"I'm serious."

"Why the cold feet all of a sudden?" she questioned. "I'm costing you five hundred dollars a day. I spent nearly a thousand on clothes for San Francisco today, and I hate to tell you what the gown for Saturday is going to set you back. At that kind of price, you're entitled to a little value for your money. I was hired to do a job, and I'm doing it."

"The hell with the money," he told her. "Anyway, I hired you to protect Andrea, not hunt down Barbara."

"In the long run, we agreed that it's the best way to get the job done. Besides, I'm the expert. You're the guy paying for the expertise." She took another bite.

She seemed not to understand his concern. Wasn't it obvious how much he cared? "Sydney, I don't want anything to happen to you."

She put down her fork. "I'm not eager for anything to happen, either—other than getting the job done."

"Just forget the job for a minute, okay?"

Sydney let out a long sigh. "Zinn, what's gotten into you? Just because we know who Barbara is, and that she's from San Francisco, is no reason to come unglued."

He drummed his fingers on the table, staring at her. He was beginning to get a little angry at her intransigence.

She pointed to his plate. "You haven't eaten a thing."

"I'm not hungry."

She grimaced, showing her own exasperation. "All right. What are you trying to say?"

He contemplated her, hesitating over whether he should tell her what was on his mind. "I don't know what impression you got this evening about my feelings for you, Sydney, but I happen to like you a lot." He shifted in his chair. "Let me rephrase that. My feelings for you are very special."

She smiled wryly. "I did get that impression." She reached over and put her hand on his. "And the feeling is mutual."

He grasped her hand and lifted it to his lips, kissing her fingers. "I couldn't live with myself if anything happened to you."

"Nothing's going to happen to me, Zinn."

"Have you already forgotten? Tonight Barbara practically ran you down."

"But she didn't."

"Sydney," he pressed, his anger really beginning to boil, "why are you being so pigheaded? Don't you see this thing has gotten out of control? It's not a joke. It's serious business."

"I've never considered it a joke. Not for one minute. And I'll be honest with you. A part of me *is* scared. I'm not indifferent to what's going on. But this is my job. This is what I do for a living."

He was struggling to control the pressure he felt. It was tough. He got up and paced back and forth. Sydney watched him. Finally he stopped behind his chair and leaned on the back of it as he stared directly at her. "I want you off the case. Jack can protect Andrea until the police take care of Barbara. I'll give you two weeks' pay, plus a bonus. Maybe you can take your mother to Hawaii at my expense until this blows over. I'll have Judy announce our breakup to the press."

Sydney couldn't believe what she was hearing. She stared at him for a long, silent moment. "You can't do that."

"Well, I am. I've decided."

She felt stung, even though she knew his intent was to protect her. Nevertheless, what he was doing upset her so much, she could hardly speak. She took a drink of water, trying to calm herself, then looked back at Zinn. "If you've lost confidence in me, fine," she said, trying to stay in control. "I can take being fired. But I refuse to be dismissed for reasons having nothing to do with my performance on the job."

He ignored her comments. "You can keep the clothes. We'll go someplace after this is over. Premieres happen all the time. I'll take you to the next one. But right now, I'd prefer you to be as far from here as possible."

"Zinn! I'm not worried about clothes or money or premieres."

"Neither am I. It's your safety I'm concerned about."

"My safety wasn't such a big deal before. What's changed?"

Zinn's expression got even harder. "Isn't that obvious?"

"Our making love has nothing to do with it. If I'd known that I was going to be treated like a china doll just because I got involved with you romantically, then I'm sorry I did it! What kind of respect could you possibly have for me if you think I'm suddenly too fragile to do my job?"

"That's not my thinking and you know it."

"What *is* your thinking? That it's all right for a woman to take on a dangerous job unless she's your girlfriend?"

"That's unfair," he protested.

"Do you deny it?"

His eyes flashed again. "I happen to care about you!"

"If you care about me, respect my dignity. Don't try and mollycoddle me. This is my work, Zinn! It's my life. My profession."

"Let me understand what you're saying. I either take you with gun in hand, or not at all?"

Sydney stared at him, hearing something she didn't like one little bit. Though the situation was different, she was hearing Dick Charles telling her mother that he wanted her—but on *his* terms. Her father had been selfish and insensitive. He'd wanted Lee, but what *she* wanted and needed counted for nothing. And her mother had accepted him under his terms and conditions. Sydney had long ago resolved never to be that way with a man. Never!

"What I'm saying, Zinn," she continued, "is you either accept me as I am, or not at all."

He stepped back and leaned against the counter, folding his arms over his chest. "It appears I've completely misread the situation."

She swallowed hard. "Maybe *I* have, too. It was probably a mistake to go to bed with you. People should never mix their personal and professional lives."

Zinn looked sad again—the way he had after they left the Hard Rock Café. He was thinking about something—she had no idea what. He sighed deeply. "All right. There's no reason your professional dignity should suffer because of what happened between us. As far as I'm concerned, you were hired to do a job. I expect you to complete it."

Sydney permitted a little smile to creep across her face. He probably didn't understand how important this outcome was to her, but at least he had the wisdom and generosity to accede to her wishes. "I appreciate you doing this. I really do."

"I guess what this means is that our . . . friendship is on hold," Zinn replied somberly.

"Under the circumstances, it's probably for the best." She was trying hard to sound levelheaded and dispassionate, but his power play had wounded her. She'd made the mistake of letting her guard down. And Zinn, being the man he was, had taken it as a sign of weakness.

"I hope you recognize the fact that I meant well." His tone was vaguely defensive.

"Yes, I realize that."

"Good. I may have jumped to conclusions, but I didn't mean to offend you."

"Don't worry about it."

Zinn watched her, feeling a terrible sense of déjà vu. Monica had been so obsessed with her career that she'd found his love insufficient compensation, too. Nothing he could do was enough. Did every woman these days put her career first? Or did he feel some sort of perverse attraction to those who did?

Just then he heard Yolanda coming in the front door. Feeling a bit like he'd been kicked in the teeth, Zinn returned to the table and began to eat his dinner.

THE NEXT MORNING SYDNEY got up wondering if she'd won the battle, but lost the war. It was still too early to tell whether the incident in the kitchen had been an aberration—a result of Zinn's natural instinct to take charge and protect—or an indication of a fundamental problem. Once Barbara was arrested, would their problems be behind them, or would there still be a conflict of interests? Much as she hated to believe it, Sydney was afraid that Zinn wanted her—but only on his terms.

By the time she'd dressed and made it to the kitchen, she discovered that Zinn had already gone to the studio for work on scenes that had been rescheduled because of his absences during the previous few days. Yolanda told her he'd gotten Andrea up to say goodbye and explain that he'd be going away for a little while. The message he'd left for Sydney was succinct: Their departure for San Francisco was set for three that afternoon; he'd have a limo pick her up at one, and he'd meet her at the airport.

Around nine, Andrea came to Sydney's room. She was in a pink jogging suit and Yolanda had done her hair in a ponytail. Sydney could tell the little girl was unhappy, because of the long look on her face.

"Daddy's going on a trip and I can't go," she said, pouting.

"I'm afraid that's true, honey. But he'll only be gone a few days."

"Are you staying home—with me?"

"No, I've got to go on the trip and help your daddy."

"Why can't I come?"

She motioned for Andrea to come sit beside her on the bed. Sydney put her arm around her. "I've got to help your daddy in San Francisco. We'll be back soon. Then maybe we can all do something special together."

Andrea was somewhat mollified, and looked particularly pleased when Sydney asked her to help her get ready. She seemed unusually clingy, so more than once Sydney stopped her packing to sit down and give her an extra-long hug.

They talked about various things, including mothers. Sydney told her how she saw her mother all the time and that they were good friends.

"Someday can I go with you to see your mommy?"

"Sure, honey. I know she'd love to see you."

That notion seemed to please her. Andrea's spirits rose, and after a while she told Sydney about a surprise Zinn had arranged for her that afternoon. Sydney asked her what it was, but the child said she didn't know, only that it was going to be very special.

Soon after she'd finished packing, a detective who worked with Kaslow came out to take a statement from her. Sydney sat with him at the kitchen table, going over the facts. There wasn't a lot to tell; the entire incident had taken only a few seconds.

At about eleven, while Andrea was playing quietly in her room, Jack Dowd showed up, a weekend suitcase and a garment bag in his hands. He had seen the publicity that Judy Meecham had been getting out and right away he remarked on what he'd read.

"I was wondering why Garrett hired you after all the work I'd done for him over the years," he chided. "Now I understand."

"Believe me, Jack, for every advantage there is to being a woman in this business, there are two disadvantages."

"Well, once the wacko is picked up, you can always marry Garrett."

"Typical male approach to the issue," she snapped.

Jack Dowd blinked. "I say something wrong, or what?"

"The subject is not a very pleasant one at the moment. Let's leave it at that."

At noon a clown named Crackers appeared at the gate with a bag of magic tricks. He was the surprise Zinn hoped would raise Andrea's spirits. Jack went down to the gate to chat with the fellow before letting him in. Sydney was glad to see he was cautious.

The limo came in the middle of Crackers's performance, which was what Zinn had intended. Sydney gave Andrea a quick kiss and a hug, and slipped away without so much as a tear being shed. Zinn's thoughtfulness was certainly a contrast to the callousness shown by her own father.

They arrived at Los Angeles Airport before Zinn and most of the crew. An airline representative escorted Sydney to a VIP lounge. During the brief time she'd spent in the lobby of the crowded terminal building she'd been acutely aware of the people moving around her. Barbara, she reminded herself, could strike at any time. Yet there were certain dangers that couldn't be guarded against. All she really could do was stay alert.

Sydney was escorted to the gate twenty minutes before departure time, and Zinn still hadn't shown up. Most of the tech crew had arrived, and some of the talent, but not the key people. The airline representative told her that the rest might have to take a later flight.

Boarding was nearly complete, and Sydney had almost resigned herself to flying alone, when Zinn and a few others came running along the concourse. "Whew!" he exclaimed. "Thought we wouldn't make it."

He slipped his arm around her shoulder and introduced her to the regular members of the cast. A couple of the faces were familiar from the TV screen. Seeing the camaraderie among them, Sydney was reminded of her youth, when her mother had taken her to see the famous and beautiful people on the studio lots.

Patti Lind, a tall, voluptuous brunette in the mold of Rosalind Russell, was particularly friendly. She played Grant Adams's assistant on the show and was loaded with panache and self-assurance. The three of them walked down the ramp together. Listening to their chatter, Sydney had a sense of not belonging.

She didn't feel neglected, though. Zinn was very solicitous. They sat side by side in the first-class cabin. Patti took her seat with the assistant director, two rows up.

"So, did Crackers show up?" Zinn asked.

"Yes. I meant to tell you how thoughtful that was. Andrea was thrilled. Hardly noticed I was leaving."

Zinn absently ran a finger along her forearm. "That was the purpose."

He was behaving as though nothing had happened between them—which, in a way, came as a relief. He was acting, of course. For once, though, it was welcome.

"The shooting schedule is pretty intense," Zinn told her. "Beginning this evening, as a matter of fact. Don has two night locations he wants to get out of the way. We'll be at it until late. Then, tomorrow morning we begin at seven."

"Nobody can accuse you of having a cushy job."

He grinned. "When you're in a series, they make you hustle."

The flight lasted only an hour, but Zinn took a catnap while Sydney paged through a magazine. He'd had a long day, so she didn't really blame him. Still, it amazed her how easily he'd slid back into the mood of the way things were before they'd made love. It was what she wanted, true; but couldn't he at least show a little difficulty in forgetting last night?

She glanced over at him, seeing the man she'd made love with; seeing the man she'd wanted so badly without admitting it—even to herself. She could feel herself weaken again. She told herself that she couldn't let herself slip back into that mode; it had very nearly been fatal.

SAN FRANCISCO WAS FOGGY that evening, but the technical people decided they could shoot anyway. A fleet of limousines and taxis delivered them to the Fairmont Hotel on Nob Hill. There was only time for a hurried meal in the coffee shop before the entire crew and Sydney headed off for Aquatic Park, the first location on the schedule.

Zinn was in good spirits, treating her as he might a live-in girlfriend, which was the role she'd been assigned. The line separating reality from pretense seemed blurred, and at times it was hard to know who she really was.

Though it was the middle of summer, a foggy evening in San Francisco was never warm. Sydney hugged herself against the cold and watched the director and actors on the set. They were about ready to do a take.

Staring at the scene, she remembered an occasion years earlier when her mother had taken her to the studio to see her father act. It was the only time she'd seen Dick Charles at work, and it had been both an exciting and upsetting experience. It had been on a soundstage, rather than an exterior location, but the memories came back to her all the same. . . .

A voice called for quiet and a hush fell over the soundstage, which was set up like a bedroom from the olden days. There was a great canopied bed, big high-backed chairs and heavy velvet draperies. Her father came onto the set wearing an old-fashioned dressing gown and a big mustache for the role, but she knew him by her mother's reaction. She had squeezed Sydney's hand excitedly, and when Sydney looked up at her mother's face, she saw that her eyes were shimmering, and heard her sigh.

Dick appeared oblivious to their presence. Or at least he acted as though he was. Sydney felt a terrible dis-

tance from him. He might as well have been on the
screen. Was that man really her father? she wondered.

After several moments, someone shouted, "Action!" and the cameras began to roll.

Dick Charles walked over to another man in a frock
coat, shouted for him to leave, then took him by the
arm and gave him a shove toward the door, which he
exited. The two ladies in long dresses watched in horror. Dick ordered the older one to leave and he was left
alone with a very pretty young one in a yellow dress,
who seemed very frightened.

Though Sydney knew it was just pretend, a movie,
she understood the girl's feelings. But when Dick held
the actress in his arms, Sydney realized that it was his
character's daughter in the film, and that he really loved
her. Though Sydney was quite young, encountering her
father at such distance had been very upsetting. When
a voice called "Cut!" and the action ceased, she managed to pull free of her mother's hand and run from the
set....

Sydney didn't think her mother had ever understood her reaction that day. It had been a long time ago,
and yet it was every bit as real as the present drama being played out before her now, in San Francisco. She
turned and looked behind her where the police had put
up a barricade to keep the spectators back. A sizable
crowd had gathered.

Sydney surveyed the faces, looking for the telltale
head of red hair. Though it was questionable that Barbara would have learned the details of the shooting
schedule, it was possible. She could be among the
crowd, watching.

Sydney hoped that Barbara Walsh would show up.
She wanted to apprehend the woman and end the threat
to Andrea. It would also mean the end of her profes-

sional relationship with Zinn. They would be free to go on with their lives. The problem was, since making love with him, she was no longer sure what she really wanted—or, for that matter, what he wanted.

Zinn finished the take in which he'd been sitting on a park bench, talking to an actor playing a desperate fugitive who had information Grant Adams needed to clear his client. The director was satisfied, and Zinn walked over to Sydney. Voices of the people behind the barricade called his name and he turned and waved. He put an arm around Sydney's shoulders.

"Heck of a way to make a living, isn't it? I could be home in my slippers with my faithful dog, reading the paper or watching the evening news like the rest of the world."

"The price of fame."

"It's a dirty job, but somebody's got to do it." He laughed.

They watched the crew moving the light stanchions for a minute or two.

"Syd," he said, his arm still on her shoulder, "I need to talk to you about last night. I hope you've been able to forgive me. I may have gotten overly emotional because of some things that happened with Monica. They say people carry baggage with them from a bad marriage, and I guess that's true."

"What does Monica have to do with anything? I don't understand."

"I don't want to devalue your commitment to your job, but her single-mindedness about her career left Andrea and me in second place. It was Monica's way of avoiding intimacy, and I didn't want that to happen to us. I didn't want to see things between us skewed out of whack right from the start. I know you took what I said to be indifference toward your needs, but it wasn't.

If anything, I was being overprotective because I really care."

Zinn's speech set her back. She'd never really thought that his intentions were bad, but what he said now cast everything in a different light. Maybe it was as simple as seeing things from another point of view.

"I'm probably overly sensitive," she replied. "I'm probably a victim of my past as much as you are of yours. My mother has spent years trying to convince me to live the life she thinks is best for me, without realizing I have to choose my own way. Her intentions are good, too. But good intentions aren't really the issue. The road to hell is paved with them, they say."

"Well," Zinn said, "you're here and you're on the job, so maybe you can at least give me credit for seeing the error of my ways."

She smiled at him and nodded. How could she argue with that?

The director called from the set. "Zinn? Where'd you go, pal?"

"Coming!" He gave Sydney a kiss on the cheek. "Duty calls, Syd. I'll get back to my acting and leave you to your sleuthing."

She watched him go, feeling strange inside. It was awfully hard to be angry with him for very long. She pulled the collar of her jacket over her neck. She'd grown tired of being on the set. It brought back a lot of memories and it wasn't the context in which she liked to think of Zinn. She felt a need to distance herself from it. A walk would be nice—a chance to be alone and think. Turning, she headed up the sloping lawn, slipped through the barricade and melted into the falling darkness.

The Buena Vista Café across from the park looked warm and cheery in the mist. An Irish coffee would taste good, but she had no desire to be in a crowd. Instead of strolling idly, she elected to head back to the hotel. That way she could be alone and get some exercise at the same time.

By following the Hyde Street cable-car line, she'd eventually arrive back at the Fairmont. So she started up Nob Hill with a determined stride, thinking it just as well she turned in early and got some sleep.

Sydney had gone two or three blocks, following the tracks of the cable car, when she became aware of someone behind her, about a couple of dozen yards back. Turning, she saw it was a man. But it wasn't Zinn or anyone she recognized from the crew. The fellow was in a trench coat and his face was obscured by the shadows.

There was no way of knowing if he was following her, but as a woman as well as a detective, Sydney was sensitive to the presence of strange men with unclear intentions. For an instant she considered whether or not there might be a connection with Barbara, but she dismissed the idea as unlikely. But to be on the safe side, Sydney checked to make sure her gun was readily accessible. It was, and she was prepared to use it.

At the next corner she stopped under the streetlight and looked up and down the hill, as if she was trying to decide which way to go. The stranger, no more than thirty yards back, stopped to light a cigarette. He was smooth, but not perfect by any means. She was very suspicious now.

A cable car was at the last intersection down the hill and clanged its bell as it started toward the point where Sydney stood waiting. The man, meanwhile, hadn't moved, and she was sure he was following her. When she stepped off the curb to indicate her intention of boarding the car, the stranger began walking slowly toward the intersection.

Several moments later the cable car arrived, and as Sydney boarded she noticed the man slip between two parked cars and get on from the other side. The trolley lurched forward and began mounting the steep hill. Sydney's pulse quickened. He was following her. But why? And who was he?

She was seated at the front of the cable car. He was standing on the running board on the opposite side, looking back down the street and avoiding her eyes. Sydney had a glimpse of his beefy face and hands. There was no question in her mind that he was up to something. She decided to find out what.

Several blocks farther up the line the track turned. While the trolley paused for traffic, Sydney jumped down and walked briskly up a foggy side street. She ducked into the recessed entrance to one of the row houses and removed her gun from her purse.

The cable car had proceeded up the street. All was quiet except for the sound of footsteps. Sydney's heart was beating rapidly and her mouth went dry. Her grip tightened on the handle of the gun. Just as the man passed the opening where she had hidden, she leaped out and grabbed him from behind, thrusting the muzzle of the gun into his ear.

He gasped with surprise, but froze. He was only a few inches taller than she, but pretty heavy.

"Okay, mister," she said through her teeth, trying to sound as fierce as she could. "Tell me why you're following me, if you want to walk away under your own power."

"I don't mean . . . to harm you," he stammered, his body rigid. "I'm just keeping an eye on you. That's all."

"Why?"

"I was hired to look out for you."

"By who?"

"Mr. Garrett. He wanted me to make sure you didn't have any problems. Honest. He said keep a distance, but don't let you get into any trouble."

Sydney felt a sudden flash of anger. "Zinn hired you?"

"Yeah. Honest."

"Who are you?"

"P.I. Name's Boranski. Norm Boranski."

Sydney released her hold on the man and took the gun away from his head. "You have an ID?"

"Yeah, sure."

Sydney stepped back but kept the muzzle of the Heckler & Koch trained on him. "Take out your wallet nice and slow."

The man did, moving very carefully, as she'd instructed. He held out his state ID card for her to see. Though she could barely read it in the dark, Sydney could tell both the ID and the man were legitimate. She let her gun hand fall to her side.

"What did Zinn think he was having you save me from?"

"The Walsh woman. The redhead."

"Oh, great."

"I'm just doing what I was paid to do. It's nothing illegal."

"I know, Boranski. I'm upset with Garrett." Their conversation about good intentions came to mind, and her anger flared. Here he was, apologizing out of one side of his mouth, all the while knowing that his hired gorilla was watching over her. What a hypocrite!

"Look," the man said, "the pay's good. I hope you don't mind if I at least see you to wherever you're going. I do my job, I get paid."

"I was just going back to the hotel."

"We can catch the next car. There'll be one in another fifteen minutes."

Sydney started back along the sidewalk. Norm Boranski followed. "I think I'll walk, if you don't mind."

"It's quite a climb up to Nob Hill."

"You said the money's good, Boranski. Besides, I can use the cool air and you can probably use the exercise."

"My drill sergeant in the marine corps wasn't as hardhearted as you, lady."

Sydney laughed, but she wasn't exactly in a lighthearted mood. Zinn hadn't been completely honest with her, and she didn't like that at all.

8

SYDNEY WATCHED TELEVISION until midnight, waiting for Zinn to return to the hotel. She figured he would wonder what had happened to her, and come to her room to find out. But it was now so late, she concluded he may have gone on to bed. So she undressed, slipped into her oversize Dodgers T-shirt, brushed out her hair and pulled back the covers.

When she went to the window to close the drapes, the magnificent view of the bay and the lights of the city caught her eye. On the sixteenth floor, they were above most of the fog that rolled through the Golden Gate and flowed over the hills from the west. It was comparatively clear out over the bay, though in the financial district below Nob Hill, fog nestled among the buildings like a layer of gauze.

Sydney began to pull the heavy drapes closed when there was a soft knock at her door. She went to it and asked, "Who is it?"

"Zinn."

"I'm ready for bed. I'm not dressed."

"I need to talk to you, Syd," said the muffled voice. "Please open up."

She pulled the door open.

Zinn stood there, his hands on his hips, looking thoroughly annoyed. "Where the hell did you disappear to? I was worried to death about you." He walked past her into the room.

Sydney closed the door, shoving it hard enough that the slam caught Zinn's attention and he turned around. "You've got some nerve," she told him.

"No. You've got nerve. I didn't find your disappearing act funny at all. There's a madwoman loose out there, determined to get you, and you waltz off as though nobody would care or notice."

Now it was Sydney's turn to put her hands on her hips. "Perhaps I should have said something, but that's not the issue. I want to know why you had me followed. Not five minutes before this gorilla starts tailing me, you're apologizing to me for your overprotectiveness. What kind of hypocrite are you, anyway?"

He sat on the bed. "He was supposed to be discreet."

"Well, he was stupid, too." She faced back and forth. "At least it's refreshing to know I wasn't the only jerk you've hired."

"Sydney..."

"I feel completely humiliated. Lied to. Tricked. How can I ever believe a word you say?"

"I hired Boranski from L.A., before we even made love. I wasn't aware of your sensitivities then."

"Well, you could have fired him, couldn't you?"

Zinn shrugged helplessly. "Jack recommended him. Besides, it was done. I figured it wouldn't do any harm."

"Jack was in on this too? He knew you were protecting me, while I was trying to protect you?" She threw up her hands in rage. "What humiliation!" She walked around the bed and stood right in front of him, glaring. "Do you know what that's like? It's like your director hired another actor to shoot your scenes over, just in case you bombed. How would you feel about *that?*"

"Sydney, if you'll calm down, you'll realize it has nothing to do with your professional ability, or my confidence in you."

She brushed the argument aside. "I didn't see you worrying that some harm might come to Norm Boranski when you hired *him* to look after me. He was in a lot more danger than I was. I could have blown his head off tonight!"

"I don't happen to feel the same way about him that I feel about you!" He got up. "Has it ever occurred to you that I just might love you, Sydney, and that it's very, very important to me that nothing happens to you?"

She started to reply, to expose the folly of his argument, when his words sank in. He'd said he loved her. Her mouth sagged open, but nothing came out.

Zinn stepped over to her. He took her by the shoulders, kneading her flesh through the light fabric of the T-shirt. She felt the slightest twinge in her sore shoulder, but it wasn't bad. Zinn's touch felt so good. The scent of the outdoors, the fog, the night air, was on his clothes. Under it was a hint of his cologne; but mostly it was nature, and it amplified his manliness.

"That's what all this is about," he said, peering into her eyes.

She gazed up at him. Her lips parted. Zinn didn't say anything more. He didn't have to. He'd already neutralized her anger. Mistakes made in the name of love, she realized, were more easily forgiven.

"This hasn't been an easy relationship for me," he said, the corners of his mouth curving slightly. "I've been hit on the head, had my profession savaged, my character impugned, my life reorganized, my heart stolen, and on top of everything, I'm told I'm a monster for trying to spare you from harm."

"I never called you a monster, Zinn." Her voice was very gentle.

He slid his hands down her arms. "The worst part has been thinking that for all I've gone through, you don't have nearly the same regard for me."

"I've never said that. I went to bed with you, didn't I? Some women may do that lightly, but I certainly don't. If I didn't have strong feelings for you, I'd never have done it. I would have thought that was self-evident."

"So self-evident that if my feelings for you raise the tiniest question about the sanctity of your work, I get sent to the corner." He lifted her fingers to his face, pressing them to his cheeks. His skin was still cool from the night air. He looked into her eyes, then turned her hands over and kissed her palms.

Sydney shivered.

Zinn put his hands on her waist, clamping it tightly. His fingers dug deeply into her skin, right through the fabric. He stared into her eyes, his expression determined.

Their bodies were inching closer. She could feel her heart start to pound against the wall of her chest. He lowered his hand to the bottom of her T-shirt.

"How's that hip of yours?"

"It's okay. A little tender, that's all."

"I'll do my best not to bump it."

Their faces were close and his lips parted slightly. Sydney reached up, put her arms around his neck, and he kissed her.

Zinn kissed her more forcefully then, pressing himself firmly against her. His hand moved up under the hem of her shirt and he traced the curve of her derriere and her bare back.

Sydney opened her mouth wider, and her tongue darted out to touch his lips and teeth. She savored the flavor of his kiss, the pressure of his body against hers.

She wanted him. She wanted his kisses, she wanted his arms around her. His strength excited her. She wanted his love, his body—every bit of him.

He'd slid his hand up her side, and then to her right breast, which he cupped in his palm. "This is all I've thought about since last night," he murmured. "I want you again, Syd. I want you badly."

Her nerves were tingling like high-voltage wires as Zinn took the bottom of her shirt and lifted it over her head in one motion. She was naked except for her bikini panties. He caressed her breasts, then bent over and circled one hard nipple with his tongue. The sensation made her breast throb so intensely that it hurt. And when he kissed the other one, she crushed his head hard against her.

Zinn lifted her into his arms and carried her to the bed, putting her down carefully. She lay watching him undress. Her eyes moved up and down his body, from his dark auburn hair to his erection. Sydney felt herself moisten as she recalled the feel of him inside her body. She craved the sensation again.

He lay down beside her, his body gently coming up against hers. Sydney felt his breath on her eyelids as he lightly kissed her face. Then his lips wandered down her nose and across to her ear. He blew softly into her ear, making her shiver. When he ran his tongue down her neck to her collarbone, she moaned.

She lay with her eyes closed, drinking in the sensations, feeling his fingers toying with the strands of her hair, fanned out across the pillow.

"You're so beautiful," he whispered. "So very lovely."

She opened her eyes and stared into his. "You are, too," she said, touching his cheek with her fingertip.

He kissed her hand, taking the tips of several fingers into his mouth. Then, slowly, he ran his finger down her chest to her navel and beyond. She held her breath as he lowered his head to caress her nipples, again sending spasms through her body.

There was an urgent pang between her legs, and another rush of hot liquid. He seemed to sense what she wanted, because he drew his prickly tongue down to her stomach. Then he began planting soft kisses from her naval to her dewy curls.

When Zinn parted her legs and lowered his head, her heart shuddered with expectation. The first kiss was so soft that she wasn't sure whether it was his lips touching her or his breath. But in a moment or two she felt the raspy sweep of his tongue. He teased her, licked her, parting her with his fingers as his kiss deepened. Waves of excitement built inside her and she knew without a doubt that she'd never wanted a man more in her life.

Sydney spread her legs even wider, wanting all of him, needing him inside her. But he continued to caress with his tongue. Her longing was almost painful, but it was *exquisitely* painful. She wanted to feel like this—poised on the hard edge of desire—forever.

Just as she was about to come, Zinn pulled away. She urged him to continue.

"Don't stop now. Please don't stop, Zinn," she pleaded.

"I have to make sure you're protected, honey," he said. He got out of bed, picked up his pants and took a condom from his pocket. After he'd put it on, he returned and took her in his arms again.

Sydney reached down to fondle him, to return the pleasure he had given her. He was long and hard, and she wrapped her fingers around him. In the shadows she could see his face, and she kissed him.

Zinn climbed over her. She guided him to her center and he slid easily inside. Almost at once he began driving into her with long, smooth strokes, faster and faster, until finally neither of them could delay the ultimate pleasure any longer.

When he couldn't hold back, he exploded inside her. His body heaved hard against her, he shuddered, and sank slowly down onto her. He stayed there for a long moment before he rolled them both onto their sides. They faced each other, still coupled, the air creeping into the narrow gap between their moist skin. Zinn brushed her hair away from her face and kissed her nose. She clung to him, her heart banging in her chest.

They lay like that for a very long time. When at last he softened and slid out of her, she couldn't hold back a sad moan of deprivation. "That was wonderful, Zinn," she breathed. "Just wonderful."

"Is it safe to say you've forgiven me?"

"I guess that's a fair assumption."

He kissed the damp hair at her temple. "You're fabulous, Syd. I love you. I really do."

She closed her eyes and held him against her, nuzzling her face into the crook of his neck. "I wish it could go on like this forever. I wish tomorrow would never come."

"Who knows?" he said, stroking her hair. "It might be even better tomorrow."

She mustered enough energy to shake her head. "No, it's not possible."

They fell silent then, content in each other's embrace. Reality hardly had meaning beyond their bed. After a while she began running her hand over his stomach. When she strayed farther down, she found him erect again. The discovery made her begin to pulse with desire and in minutes they were making love. This time she sat astride him, her hips undulating against his rock-hard loins as he caressed her breasts.

After they'd come again, they each dozed off into a contented sleep. A couple hours later she awoke to his kisses. She was surprised to discover that even in sleep her body hadn't lost its seemingly unquenchable desire for him. This time they made love in several different positions—with her legs resting on his shoulders, on their sides facing each other, and finally from behind with her haunches thrust into his loins.

"Oh, God," she moaned after he'd climaxed. "Don't be surprised if you wake up and find me blissfully dead. Maybe I already am and I don't know it."

"If so, I am, too. And this is heaven."

"I think that must be it," she purred.

He kissed her neck and she cuddled against him.

"How could I ever be mad at you?" she whispered, her words dying on her lips. If he answered, she didn't hear him. In minutes she was fast asleep.

SYDNEY HADN'T SLEPT SO soundly in months. She awoke around seven, but Zinn was already gone. She didn't know when he'd slipped away, but it had to be early morning, because he'd stayed with her through most of the night.

She was sore from their night of lovemaking. She'd never experienced anything like that before—pleasure on top of pleasure. Zinn was much more than a heartthrob, he was an accomplished lover. He knew how to satisfy her in every way.

Sydney shivered with ecstasy at the recollection of the things he'd done. It was a once-in-a-lifetime experience, a fantasy that seemed impossible to duplicate.

And yet there was no reason to believe it wouldn't happen again and again and again.

Much as she enjoyed their lovemaking, though, the next day always brought a measure of uncertainty. There were problems that sex alone, even terrific sex, couldn't resolve. They had glossed over their differences because of their overpowering attraction to each other. In the cold light of morning, Sydney knew they had problems to face.

True, Zinn had apologized. He'd made a genuine effort to communicate with her, to explain the reasons for his actions. But how could she be sure he truly understood her sensitivity? He'd said he loved her, but it wasn't really his motivation that troubled her. It was his underlying attitudes and philosophy.

Zinn had justified himself by explaining that Monica had been obsessed with her career. Sydney didn't know the details of the marriage, naturally, but how out of line had the woman been? Could Zinn himself have been overly demanding or unreasonable?

Sydney had no intention of defending Zinn's ex-wife against him, but by the same token his experience wasn't irrelevant to their own relationship. He'd said as much himself.

Of course, in time everything would become clear. There was always the danger, though, that they would get so wrapped up in their mutual attraction that fundamental issues would get swept under the carpet. As the events of the night before came back to her, Sydney could see how easy it would be to brush aside their differences and live for the moment.

More than one couple had waited until they were committed or even married before they began addressing problems that should have been worked out in advance. That could even have been a mistake Zinn had made with Monica.

Sydney looked over at the pillow where his head had been. With him beside her, the thoughts troubling her now had been the furthest thing from her mind. So, why was she fastening on them now? Was she afraid to enjoy the experience? Afraid of the day when it wouldn't always be so idyllic?

Maybe it was fear, or maybe she was too much of a realist. Her mother had often told her that, though not in quite those words.

"Sydney, darling," she'd say, "where's the romance in your soul? Why do you insist on calculating everything to the nth degree? To live is to let your heart go free!"

It was no secret why she'd rejected her mother's philosophy. Lee's notion of romance was clinging to the dream Dick Charles had dangled before her. Long ago, Sydney had decided that wasn't the way she wanted to live her life.

She sat up on the edge of the bed and looked around the room that had been the scene of the most sensual night of her life. How many women would say she was crazy to be grousing? Her mother certainly would.

Of course, it had probably been on such night that Sydney herself had been conceived. Her mother had thrown caution to the wind and pursued the romance in her soul on at least that one occasion. No doubt her father had professed words of love. And maybe he'd even meant them at the time. But that couldn't change the fact of who Dick Charles was. It didn't even matter that Dick and Lee shared careers and aspirations; they lacked shared values.

The unanswered question was whether she had anything in common with Zinn Garrett besides a healthy libido.

She got up and paced around the room, asking herself why she felt obliged to talk herself out of something that was wonderful. *Fear.* That was the only answer.

And if she was afraid, what was Zinn thinking? That everything was wonderful? That after a day of shooting they'd come back to the hotel and do it all over again? But why had he gone off and left her sleeping? Because he wanted her safe in the hotel?

Sydney sat down and put her head in her hands. She knew she was being stupid. Until she talked with Zinn, she wouldn't know how he felt. She'd get dressed and then try and track him down. Maybe they could talk about it.

She went off to the bathroom for a soak in the tub. On the vanity she found a note from Zinn:

Syd,
Several of us are planning dinner this evening. Patti's guy is flying in tonight and Elliot's wife will be here this morning. Put on one of those new outfits and we'll do the town.

Hope you aren't upset with me for not waking you. You were sleeping so peacefully. Anyway, this morning's shoots will be a drag. I'll call you at lunchtime. We're doing a beach location this afternoon, if that interests you.

Did I tell you last night how beautiful and wonderful you are? If I forgot, I'll tell you this evening.
Love, Zinn

Sydney read the note twice more before putting it back where she'd found it. He sounded so sincere. It made her question her skeptical mind. Yet she knew it didn't matter how sincere he was. What mattered was who they each were.

When she'd finished bathing, she dressed and ordered a room-service breakfast. While sipping her coffee she looked out at the bay, thinking it a shame that she wasn't able to relax and enjoy what could have been a fabulous romantic tryst.

Ironically, the person who should have interfered with the enjoyment—Barbara Walsh—hadn't surfaced. Was it possible she hadn't taken the bait? Sydney hated to think that Barbara was still in L.A.—or worse, that she might have refocused her attention on the little girl.

Just thinking about Andrea reactivated her concerns. Sydney decided to give her a tingle and went to the phone to dial Zinn's number in Pacific Palisades. Yolanda answered the phone.

"Oh, *señorita*, it's so good to hear your voice. The *niña*, all she do is talk about you and her daddy. As soon as the clown, he go, the talk, it start."

"I thought that might happen. That's why I called. Do you want to put her on the line?"

"She's watching *Sesame Street*, but for you she would leave the Big Bird, I know. I get her. You wait, okay?"

Sydney could hear Yolanda putting the phone down. A moment later she heard someone else picking it up. "Sydney, that you? This is Jack."

"Oh, hi, Jack. How's it going?"

"I've managed to avoid Bert and Ernie, if that's what you mean."

Sydney laughed. "It's a dirty job, Jack, but somebody's got to do it."

"One thing, though, I thought I'd mention while the maid's out of the room."

"Yeah?"

"You know anybody who's getting married, by any chance?"

"Married? What are you talking about?"

"Funny thing. This morning I go down to get the paper and there's this doll hanging on the front gate. A bride doll."

"A bride doll?"

"Yeah, like little girls play with, only this one's kind of fancy and old looking. But that's not all. It's got a note pinned to it that says, 'Nice dress.' That's all, just 'Nice dress.' Oh, yeah, and something else. There's some red ink on the front of the dress and a straight pin sticking in it, voodoo-style. I figured it could be the work of the wacko, but I don't understand why the bride doll. What do you make of it?"

Sydney immediately thought of the dress she had picked out at Nola's. "I think it's the dress that's important, Jack, and I'm pretty sure it's the work of Barbara. What I don't understand is how she knew about it."

"I don't follow."

"Never mind. It doesn't matter. Have you mentioned anything about it to Yolanda?"

"No, I didn't want to get her all upset."

"Good. Hang on to the doll. I want to see it." Sydney looked at her watch. "I'm going to try to catch a flight back to L.A. I'll be there in a couple of hours."

"I thought you had to stay in San Francisco for three days."

"Barbara's down there, apparently, so why stay on here? Anyway, Zinn's busy."

"Does that mean I get to leave *Sesame Street?*"

She laughed. "No, Jack, I'm afraid not. I've been itching to go on the offensive. This may be my chance."

"Thanks loads. Oops, here comes the kid. I'll put her on."

She could hear Andrea's squeals in the background, followed by her excited voice on the phone. "Sydney, Sydney, when are you coming home?"

"Maybe today, honey, if I can."

"Daddy, too?"

"No, but he'll be home pretty soon."

Sydney spent a few minutes chatting with Andrea, then got off the phone. She called the concierge in the lobby and asked to be booked on the first possible flight leaving for LAX. Then she jotted out a brief note for Zinn, saying only that there was a new lead in L.A. that required her prompt attention and that she'd call him that night. After stuffing the note in an envelope, she threw her things in her suitcase and headed for the elevator, pausing long enough to slip the note under Zinn's door.

SYDNEY CAUGHT A TAXI at LAX. In half an hour she was pulling up in front of Zinn's. The driver asked if she wanted any help with her bags, but she assured him she could handle them herself. Two minutes later she was ringing the doorbell. Yolanda answered.

They'd hardly gotten out their hellos when there was a yelp in the hallway and Andrea made a beeline for her, not unlike the way she'd greeted Zinn that first day she'd visited. The two of them hugged in the hallway, Andrea squealing with glee. Sydney picked her up.

Jack Dowd, in stocking feet, with a soft-drink can in his hand, came moseying along from the direction of the kitchen. At the sight of him, Sydney saw Yolanda roll her eyes.

"That man eat too much," the housekeeper said under her breath. "I have to go to the grocery store just for him! *¡Dios mio!*"

Sydney laughed. "That's probably why Zinn hired me," she whispered. "To save on the food bill."

"Howdy," Jack said, bringing his hulking body to a halt before them. "How's Frisco?"

"Foggy."

Andrea began yammering away and Sydney put her down.

"How about if I come see you in your room in a minute, sweetheart. Right now I have to talk to Mr. Dowd."

Yolanda took the protesting child off to her room and Sydney went with Jack into the den. He went to the liquor cabinet and pulled out the doll he'd told her about on the phone. Sydney examined it.

"This is an antique."

"Yeah?"

"Not cheap, either. The uncanny thing is how much it resembles my dress."

"What dress?"

"One I bought for a premiere I'm going to with Zinn this weekend."

"How would the wacko know that?"

"That's something I'd like to know."

"So, what do you make of her hanging it on the gate? Another threat?"

"Probably." Sydney examined the doll. "You haven't notified the police, have you?"

"Since you said you were coming back right away, I figured you could take care of it."

"Good. I think I'll give Marvin Kaslow a call." She got up. "Thanks for the way you handled this, Jack."

He shrugged. "Glad something happened. I was getting bored, to be honest."

"Just stay alert. Barbara still might have plans for Andrea."

"Personal security is my thing, doll. I know this end of the business."

Sydney nodded. "If I'd have been Zinn, I'd have hired you."

"So, why do you suppose he didn't?"

She headed for the door, the antique bride doll in hand. "Because I adore *Sesame Street*, old buddy."

Before going in to see Andrea, Sydney tried to reach Kaslow. He was at his desk in the Glass House downtown when she called.

"Thought you were up north," he said, sounding surprised to hear her voice.

"The action seems a little hotter down here. I take it you haven't picked up Barbara Walsh yet."

"Not yet, kiddo," the detective said, his New York accent strong. "We tracked down her family in a San Francisco suburb, but they've been looking for her, too. Said a few months ago she flipped out, then disappeared. They're worried. Talked to the shrink who'd been treating her. He's afraid she's reached the violent stage."

"Tell me about it."

"Yeah, right. Guess you've seen for yourself."

"You haven't had any luck tracing her?"

"She's been using credit cards, so we've found out where she's been sleeping and eating. But always after the fact. She's a wily character. Manages to stay a step ahead of us."

"What's your most recent fix on her?"

"Pasadena, two nights ago. But she's in and out of Hollywood, too."

As she talked, Sydney was examining the doll. On the inside of the dress she noticed a label from Granny's Attic, an antique shop on Melrose Avenue. "Any idea what she's driving these days?"

"The rental car was abandoned. Her prints were all over it, so we know we've got the right suspect. No idea what she's driving now, though. Could have stolen or borrowed wheels. Who knows?"

"I assume you've got an APB out on her."

"Yeah, every law-enforcement agency in the state has got her mug. This morning the brass decided to go public with it. She'll be in the papers this afternoon."

"With all the publicity, she can't hide for long."

"That's what I figure."

"I don't know if it means much," Sydney said, "but I've got something else you might want to check on." She explained the doll and gave him the name and address of the shop on Melrose.

"Yeah," Kaslow replied. "Sounds like something we ought to look into. I'll get somebody on it when I get a chance."

"Doesn't sound like you think it will lead to anything."

He let out an audible sigh. "It's not that, Sydney. We're pretty pressed for man-hours, as it is. If this was really hot, I'd shift somebody onto it, but right now I've got two teams checking motels, and this ain't our only crime, either."

"Maybe I'll poke around, then."

"I'm not saying I won't do anything," Kaslow protested.

"Consider it volunteer assistance. No charge."

"I'd feel better if you'd leave this to us," he said plaintively.

Sydney didn't want to annoy Kaslow, because she needed his cooperation. But she wasn't going to abdicate her responsibility to her client, either. "I'll keep a low profile, I promise. But there is one thing you could do for me, Marvin."

"What's that?"

"You must have a picture of Barbara by now. It'd help if I knew what she looked like."

"We do have a few, yes. I suppose I could make a print available. Want me to send it over to you?"

"I'd like it sooner rather than later. How about if I come by to pick it up?"

"Sure. It'll be in a manila envelope down at Reception."

"I'll be there in an hour or so."

"Well, if you turn up something, give me a buzz, huh?"

"Sure thing." Sydney hung up, acknowledging the wisdom of Candy Gonzalez's old adage that if you need the cops to do something fast, you're probably better off doing it yourself.

Putting Barbara Walsh's voodoo doll in a sack, Sydney went to Andrea's room to give her a few minutes of her time. Afterward she was going to borrow Zinn's Jaguar, drop by to see Nola in Westwood, then head for Hollywood to visit Granny's Attic on Melrose. Since Jack was occupying the guest room, Sydney decided to take her bags with her and spend the night in Glendale with her mother.

"OH, SYDNEY," Nola Jiménez said, seeing her walk into the shop, "the dress won't be ready for at least two more days."

"Actually, that's not why I'm here. I wanted to talk to you."

Nola, a petite woman in her late fifties with dark, shining eyes, invited her into a private office at the back of the shop. She motioned for Sydney to sit in the chair opposite her small writing desk. "In less than a week, you've become my most celebrated client," she said cheerfully.

"Me?"

"Honey, you're the talk of the town. You'd think you'd just starred in a hit film. Whenever I mention to someone I'm dressing you, they always want to know what you're like. I've even had calls inquiring if I'm doing your dress."

"Who phoned?"

"A reporter."

"And they wanted to know about my dress?"

"I've had similar things before, though usually for something like a wedding dress. And I must say she— the reporter—was very strange. Asked if she could come and see it. Didn't seem to care about anybody else's gown. I'm doing at least six for this event."

"Nola, what was this reporter's name? Who did she work for?"

"She said a TV station, but I don't recall her name. It was something ordinary, like Brown or Jones or something."

"Did she come by?"

"Yes, yesterday. Came in and announced she was here to see the dress. I figured since you'd be wearing it in a couple of days, there'd be no problem. There wouldn't be time for anyone to copy it."

"What happened?"

Nola shrugged. "She looked it over and left. She was kind of rude, actually. Didn't even thank me."

"Nola, what did this woman look like?"

"She was tall, fairly attractive, but a little disheveled. I'd say thirty-five. Red hair, just about shoulder-length."

"And she acted strange?"

"Yes. A very unusual woman." Nola saw the look on Sydney's face. "Do you know her?"

"I believe we have a passing acquaintance, so to speak."

Nola's brow furrowed. "I hope you don't mind that I showed her the dress."

"No, but I think you'd better be careful if she comes back. I think she's the same woman who's been threatening Zinn Garrett's little girl."

"The kidnapper?"

"Possibly. And she may have plans to look me up, too."

"Oh, Sydney!" There was horror in Nola's voice.

"But don't worry, just give the police a call if you hear from her again."

"I will. You can be sure of that."

Sydney left Nola's, promising she'd be back to pick up her dress. As she walked to Zinn's car, she couldn't help glancing over her shoulder from time to time, half expecting to see Barbara Walsh.

Sydney was eager see what the woman looked like, even if it meant driving through rush-hour traffic to get downtown. She got on the Santa Monica Freeway and drove east to the Parker Center in the heart of the city. The envelope Kaslow promised was waiting. She tore it open at once.

The woman in the photograph was distinctive looking, with strong, even features that were a touch masculine. The picture looked as though it had been taken by a professional. Sydney stared at the eyes, which were a bit hawkish, giving the subject an eeriness that was unsettling. Slipping the photo back into the envelope, she headed for the car. If she hurried, she could make it up to Melrose Avenue, where the antique shop was located, before closing time.

9

GRANNY'S ATTIC, an antique shop on Melrose, wasn't far from Paramount Studios in Hollywood. By the time Sydney got there, it was after five. A sign in the window indicated the staff would return in fifteen minutes. Sydney decided to wait.

Most of the stock, from what she could see, appeared to be collectibles. Dolls seemed to be a specialty. Half the window display consisted of antique dolls of various types.

Sydney hadn't let her mother know she'd be spending the night with her, so, since she had time to kill, she decided to give Lee a call. She walked to the drugstore on the corner to find a pay telephone.

"Why aren't you in San Francisco?" Lee asked as soon as Sydney told her where she was.

"It's a long story, but basically I'm working on a lead."

"But, what about Zinn?"

"He'll be fine without me, Mother. I just wanted you to know I'd be with you tonight."

"Oh, Sydney, why on earth would you leave a perfectly wonderful man to play gumshoe?"

"Mom, I'll have to tell you later."

She hung up, annoyed with her mother for chastising her. But Lee had reminded her that she had brushed Zinn aside in her haste to pursue Barbara. Actually, thoughts of him had been gnawing at her all day. Sydney knew she was running from him, but she preferred not to deal with that at the moment. A little distance was what she needed until she could figure out what to do.

She didn't want to be unfair to Zinn, though. If he'd been upset when he discovered she'd left town, it would pay to soothe his ruffled nerves. She called the Fairmont in San Francisco and was told Zinn was not in his room, so she left a message that she would be at her mother's in Glendale that night.

Sydney walked back to the antique shop and found it open. A very heavy woman in her sixties, wearing a flowered print dress, was sitting in an armchair behind the counter at the rear of the shop. A bag of potato chips was in her hand.

"May I help you?" the woman asked, without bothering to get up as Sydney approached the counter.

"I have a doll that I believe was purchased here," Sydney began. "I was wondering if you might be able to tell me who bought it."

Setting the bag of chips aside, the woman struggled to her feet and came to the counter. Sydney opened the paper sack and pulled out the doll. The woman took it, examining it briefly. "This was mine, all right, but somebody's made a mess of it. I don't sell merchandise in this condition."

"Can you tell me who bought it?"

"Yes. I sold it day before yesterday to a regular customer."

"Who?"

The woman, dour-faced, stroked her double chins. "Who are you, anyway?"

"My name's Sydney Charles. I'm a private investigator." She showed the woman her ID. "I'm trying to locate the person who bought this doll."

"What's she done?"

"That's something I'd like to discuss with her."

The woman looked over the doll, thinking. "Her name's Barbara. That's about all I can tell you. She's come in off and on over the past few years, usually to buy a doll. My impression is she's a collector. This week's the first time I've seen her in a couple of months."

Sydney took the photograph she'd gotten from Kaslow from her purse. "Is this Barbara?"

The woman examined the photo. "Yes, that's her."

Sydney felt her heartbeat quicken. "Do you have any idea where I might be able to find her?"

The proprietor shook her head. "No. I asked her this last time if she wanted me to call her, but she said no, she wouldn't give me a phone number. Said she'd just come by and check."

"Check what?"

"A doll she wanted. I'd seen it at an antique show in Santa Monica. Another dealer had it. Nineteenth-century Russian. I told Barbara about it and she got all excited. It had red hair. She loves dolls with red hair. So I told her I'd get it and she could come by the shop and see it. The dealer's a friend of mine. We trade pieces all the time."

Sydney felt her adrenaline start to flow. "When did Barbara say she'd return?"

"I told her to give me a couple of days. She said she'd call tomorrow and see if it was in. It's here, by the way. Came in this afternoon."

"Listen, it's very important that I find Barbara. If she calls you, will you let me know?"

The woman frowned. "I don't want to get mixed up in anything."

"I'll make it worth your while." Sydney took a twenty-dollar bill from her wallet. "This is yours if you call me and let me know when she'll be coming by. If I'm able to connect with her, you'll get two more twenties."

The woman looked at the bill. "I don't know."

"All you have to do is alert me that she's on her way. And it's very important that you don't tell her about this."

"Is this on the up-and-up?"

"I assure you, it is. I want to talk to her very badly."

The woman fingered the bill. "I don't suppose a phone call would hurt. And forty more, if you're able to make contact with her?"

"Right."

"Okay, I'll do it. Where do I reach you?"

Sydney gave the woman her mother's telephone number in Glendale. "Remember, it's very important to be discreet."

DURING THE DRIVE to Glendale in rush-hour traffic, Sydney considered whether she ought to advise Marvin Kaslow of her discovery. She decided that she should. She doubted he'd go so far as staking out the shop, but if Barbara called and indicated she was going there, he'd undoubtedly send a team of detectives to arrest her.

When the traffic on the Golden State Freeway ground to a halt, Sydney thumped her fingers on the steering wheel. Rush hour was the time of day she hated most. The driver of the Porsche next to her was on his car phone, reminding her why gadgets were so popular in L.A. On the drive to the Hard Rock Café, she had noticed that Zinn kept a portable phone under the armrest. She checked, and sure enough, it was there.

Since she was sitting in traffic with nothing else to do, she tried to reach Kaslow at his office, but the detective had gone for the day. She left a message that Barbara Walsh might be visiting Granny's Attic on Melrose in Hollywood sometime the next day. Sydney indicated she would call with more specifics when she had them.

Half an hour later she pulled up in front of her mother's house in Glendale. She grabbed her luggage out of the back and headed up the sidewalk. Lee opened the front door before she could even ring the bell.

"Sydney Anne Charles," she began, using her best "mother" voice, "what have you done to that poor man? Zinn's already called three times, more upset each time than the last."

Sydney received the news with mixed feelings. She set her suitcases down and shut the door behind her. "Was he worried or angry?"

"It was hard to say. He was polite enough to me, but it could have been either."

"Well, I guess I'd better give him a call."

Lee walked over to the telephone and stood by it, waiting.

"Mom, will you at least let me go to the bathroom first?"

"Oh, Sydney," she moaned, "how can you be so cavalier?"

"Cavalier? Everybody goes to the bathroom sometime."

"That's not what I mean and you know it."

Lee was waiting when Sydney returned to the front room a few minutes later. She looked concerned and upset.

"Are you going to tell me what's going on, or do you intend to keep me in the dark?" she asked.

"I told you—I came back to L.A. because a hot lead turned up," Sydney replied.

"I'm not referring to that silly detective business. I'm talking about your relationship with Zinn! What's happened? Does he love you? Do you love him?"

"Don't be expecting a son-in-law anytime soon—let me put it that way."

Lee tossed her head with exasperation. "Oh, Lord. Don't tell me you've discouraged him."

"I find him attractive, like virtually every other red-blooded American woman. But there's a big difference between physical attraction and love. I would have thought after all these years you would have figured that out, Mother."

"Listen, young lady, if you're referring to my feelings toward your father, you're completely out of line. You have no idea what went on between Dick and me, or how we felt, so I suggest you keep your speculation to yourself."

She'd hurt her mother's feelings, so she went over and put her arms around her. "I'm sorry, Mom. I shouldn't have said that."

"Well, I suppose it's understandable. You've suffered over the years for the decisions Dick and I made. But I really don't see what that has to do with you and Zinn Garrett. You either love each other, or you don't."

Sydney let out a long sigh. "Mother, people develop all kinds of romantic notions that simply aren't justified. We've talked about your relationship with my father ad infinitum, so there's no point in going into that. You know as well as I do, Hollywood is not your everyday place. It does things to people.

"Look at Monica. She screwed up her marriage because she was obsessed with being a star. And Barbara Walsh! She doesn't even know Zinn, yet she's making his life miserable. I ask myself if this is really something I want to get involved in."

"Sydney, you can spare me the bull. Let's get to the bottom line. Do you love him or not?"

"Well . . . I . . . care for him."

Lee had a look of pure satisfaction on her face. "All right, you love him. Next question. Are you rejecting him because he's an actor and he happens to work in Hollywood where people like Monica Parrish, Barbara Walsh and *your own mother* are running about?"

"Mom, don't say that. I shouldn't have compared you with those women. And anyway, I'm not rejecting him. I'm just not sure how I feel. I mean, I do care for him very much. But I know that's not enough."

Lee rolled her eyes. "There you go, calculating again."

"Of course, I'm calculating. It's irresponsible not to calculate. The fact remains that Zinn has his life and I have mine. Okay, I made assumptions about him at first that were unfair. They were proved wrong. But do you know how different we are? I mean, how different our lives are?"

"What are you saying? That you're unwilling to compromise?"

The telephone rang just then and they both looked at it. Sydney was annoyed by the intrusion, especially because she knew who it probably was and she had no idea what she was going to say.

"I expect it's for you," Lee said casually. "You might as well answer it." With that, she turned and headed for the kitchen.

Sydney let it ring again, then picked up the receiver. "Hello?"

"Well, you're alive. That answers my first question." It was Zinn.

"Hi. Did you get my note?"

"Sydney, what in the hell are you doing, running off and leaving me like this?"

"You got the note, but you didn't read it," she replied dryly.

"I leave you in bed, sleeping like an angel, expecting to see you in a few hours, and the next thing I know you're off somewhere spoiling for a fight with the forces of evil."

"'Spoiling for a fight with the forces of evil,' as you put it, is what you hired me to do, if you recall."

"I'm sorry, I didn't mean to be sarcastic. But can't you see how this might upset me?"

"Zinn, are we back to where we started? Are you saying you don't want me to do what I do?"

He sighed. "All right. I won't tell you that I worry, that I love you, that I want you safe. Apparently that doesn't count for much, anyway. So I'll ask you what you're doing."

"With regard to the case? Or us?"

"What I care about is us, but answer it any way you wish."

"They're related, actually. What I want to do is get Barbara off the streets. Then, when that's taken care of, I suppose we have to talk."

"Thank God for small favors."

"You're being sarcastic again."

"You're right," he said. "I apologize. Seeing as I was left with the impression we were getting along rather well, could you give me a clue what you're thinking at the moment?"

Sydney looked at the picture of her father over the fake fireplace. "That's the problem, Zinn. I don't know. I'm trying to take a long-term view of things, and I'm not sure what to think. The problem is, whenever I'm with you I get all muddled."

He laughed. "That's the first time I've heard my effect on a woman described that way, but I'll take your word for it."

She spoke very softly. "Last night was wonderful, don't get me wrong. Maybe it was too wonderful. That may be my problem."

"Sydney, your mind is a constant source of bafflement to me, but I love you anyway."

"I don't think you see the problem."

"Listen, babe, you hit the nail on the head when you said we have to talk. We'll be wrapping up shooting here tomorrow. Then I'm headed for home. You and I can talk then—for days, if that's what it takes. Why don't you go back to my place? I'll meet you there in the afternoon."

"I'd like to get the case wrapped up first. Since Jack's looking after Andrea, I think I'll just stay here. I have a feeling tomorrow we might get lucky with Barbara."

"Why? What's happened?"

"Oh, nothing I can't tell you about later. Kaslow and I may have a good lead—let me put it that way. I'll know better tomorrow."

"When can I see you, then?"

"I'll call you, Zinn. But we've got a date day after tomorrow for the premiere. If Barbara hasn't been picked up by then, we may as well go ahead with that and see if we can draw her out."

"Sounds like a fun evening."

Sydney laughed. "You want her arrested, don't you?"

"Yes, you know I do. But that's not all that I want."

His tone said as much as his words. So long as Andrea was safe, Barbara Walsh simply didn't matter anymore. What he cared about was her. "If it's any consolation," she said, "I'll be glad when this is over, too."

"Maybe then, we'll each find out what it is to be normal."

"Yes, you're probably right." Sydney realized what he'd just said was key—neither of them had really known the other under normal conditions.

SYDNEY SPENT A HORRIBLE night. When she and Barbara Walsh weren't chasing each other around a bridal shop, Zinn was in the surf, swimming for all he was worth and fighting the undertow, but unable to get to her on the beach. Just before dawn she finally fell into a deep sleep. Lee awakened her around nine-thirty.

"Sydney, look here. Look what was delivered just now."

Sydney blinked her eyes open to see her mother standing by the bed with two florist's boxes in her arms. Lee sat on the edge of the bed, laying one box on Sydney's stomach as she examined the card on the other.

"How thoughtful!" Lee exclaimed. "They're from Zinn! This one's for me. The note says, 'With a daughter so lovely, the mother can only be a beauty herself. Thank you for bringing Sydney into my life. Zinn Garrett.'"

Her mother batted her eyes. "Isn't that the most scrumptious thing you've ever heard?" She removed the ribbon and lifted the lid. "Oh, aren't they gorgeous! Pink roses!" Lee beamed. "What a delicious, thoughtful man. How charming!"

Sydney studied her mother's ebullient face. "Did my father ever send you flowers?"

The question made Lee stop. "Why, yes. When we were . . . together . . . he sent them all the time." She observed the knowing look on Sydney's face. "But that was done much more in those days. Hollywood was awash in flowers back then."

"Maybe Zinn's from the old school."

A look of pure exasperation crossed Lee's face. "How can you ridicule the man? Honestly, Sydney, you don't deserve him. You really don't!"

"I'm not ridiculing, Mother. I'm observing."

"Oh, posh! Look at you. You haven't even read the card or looked to see what you got."

Sydney did open the card—not that she hadn't been dying to. It read, "If there is tragedy in all this, it could only be that we don't love each other the way I know we could. Perhaps that is what we should talk about. Love, Zinn."

The sentiment brought a lump to her throat. Zinn seemed sensitive to her fears, he seemed to understand, and yet she was still afraid to hope. She blinked away the moisture in her eyes and tried to act blasé, though she knew it was hopeless.

"I won't ask you what it says," Lee told her. "But could I see the flowers?"

Sydney removed the ribbon and lifted the lid of the box. He'd sent an enormous mixed spring bouquet. It was gorgeous.

"How beautiful!" Lee exclaimed.

Sydney bit at her lip, but she couldn't hold back the emotion. She put the flowers down on the bed beside her and began to cry. Lee took her into her arms and stroked her back and head, just as she had when Sydney was a little girl.

"Don't worry, darling. It's natural for a woman to feel like this when she's fallen for a man. And just as natural to wrestle with her doubts."

"Why couldn't he have been an accountant, or a dentist?" she sobbed.

"He wouldn't have been the same man if he was, and you might not have loved him. Sometimes you're best off to accept things as they are," Lee said thoughtfully.

"Only if he's willing to accept me as I am."

"There are two sides to every coin, darling. You also have to ask if you're willing to accept *him* as *he* is." Lee kissed her on the temple and got up from the bed. "Shall I put our flowers in a vase?"

Sydney nodded, wiping her nose.

"Why don't you have your shower and I'll fix you some breakfast?"

Lee was clearly in her "mother" mode. Sydney had to admit, for once she didn't mind.

When Lee had gone, Sydney went into the bathroom. Several minutes later she was in the shower, shampooing her hair, when there was a loud thumping on the door.

"Sydney! Sydney!" It was her mother.

She turned off the shower, even though her hair was fully lathered with shampoo. "What, Mom?"

"There's a woman on the telephone from some antique shop. She said it's urgent that I tell you that the person you wanted to see is on her way over to pick up a doll or something. Does that make any sense?"

"Yes. Did she say when?"

"She said right away. In the next fifteen minutes or so."

"Good Lord," Sydney said under her breath. "Is she still on the phone?"

"Yes."

"Tell her to stall as long as possible. I'm on my way."

"Sydney, what's this all about?"

"I'll tell you later. I've got to get to Hollywood." Sydney turned the shower back on and hurriedly rinsed out her hair. Then she hopped out of the shower, dry-ing herself as she raced to her room. She was pulling on a pair of jeans when Lee appeared at her bedroom door.

"Does this have to do with that woman you've been trying to catch?"

"Yes, Mom. In a word, yes."

"Oh, Sydney, I wish you wouldn't...."

She slipped a T-shirt over her head, not bothering with a bra, then grabbed a pair of socks and some running shoes. "Listen," she said as she hurriedly tied her shoes, "I want you to make a telephone call for me. Try to reach a detective at L.A.P.D. headquarters named Marvin Kaslow. Tell him Barbara Walsh is going to be at the shop on Melrose in ten minutes. Tell him to get a black-and-white over there right now."

Lee was standing there, biting her thumbnail. "Oh, I wish you wouldn't do this sort of thing, darling. I really—"

"Mom," she said digging through her purse for her gun, "this is not the time to debate. Can you do what I said? It's very important."

Lee eyed the gun with trepidation. "Yes, yes. I'll call Detective Kaslow."

Sydney stuck her semiautomatic into the waistband of her jeans. She grabbed her mother by the shoulders and gave her a quick kiss. Lee's eyes looked like they were about to gush tears.

"Oh, darling, do be careful."

Sydney dashed for the door. "I will. Don't worry." She was already down the hall and, after a few quick strides across the tiny front room, she was at the front door. Throwing it open, she ran to the Jaguar. Lee didn't appear at the door until Sydney had the car in gear. As she screeched away, her mother waved goodbye, her face a mask of terror.

Sydney drove as fast as she safely could without causing undue risk to other motorists. She did roll through a couple of stop signs, co-opting the right of way, and careened around corners on her way to the freeway. The traffic was heavy, but the morning rush was over. She was able to move above the speed limit most of the way to Hollywood.

By the time she got there it had been over twenty minutes from the time her mother knocked on the door. That meant the proprietor would have had to delay Barbara several minutes, at least. But even if Sydney didn't make it to the shop in time, there was a good chance that the police would, if Kaslow was on the ball. It occurred to her, though, that her mother might have trouble getting through to the detective, and the urgency of the situation might not be evident to anyone else she spoke with.

As she approached the Melrose Avenue exit, she remembered Zinn's portable phone. She dialed her mother first. Lee answered on the first ring.

"Did you get hold of Kaslow, Mom?"

"Yes, darling, but it took a while. He was in a meeting and I told the man it was terribly urgent, but it must have taken ten minutes. When I finally talked to him, he said he'd have some officers over at the shop immediately."

"Good. I just wanted to make sure."

"Sydney, don't take any chances."

She was exiting the freeway. "I won't. Don't worry."

The traffic on Melrose seemed to be moving at a snail's pace, and every light insisted on changing just as she got there. She zoomed past Paramount Studios and began looking for the shop, which was on the other side of the street. Ahead, facing the opposite direction, was a patrol car, double-parked, its lights flashing. The police had gotten there; the only question was if it was in time.

As she approached, Sydney slowed the Jaguar. She could see two uniformed officers at the door of the shop, talking to the proprietor. The woman was pointing back up the street. Judging by the scene, Sydney figured that Barbara had already fled.

Suddenly a parked car pulled out of a space directly in front of her. Sydney slammed on the brakes, barely avoiding a collision. The errant car lurched forward, bumping the parked car in front of it as it forced its way into the traffic. Sydney sounded her horn, causing the driver to look back. It was then that she saw the red hair and piercing eyes of the woman in Marvin Kaslow's photograph. It was Barbara Walsh at the wheel!

In that brief instant it was impossible to tell whether there was recognition, or Barbara was simply in a panic to escape. In either case, she sped off. Sydney put the Jaguar in gear and took off in pursuit. As she passed the patrol car and the shop, she honked her horn, catching the attention of the officers, though she wasn't sure they realized what was happening.

There was hardly time to stop and talk unless she wanted to risk losing Barbara, so she continued after the fugitive. At Highland Avenue, Barbara made a left against the light, nearly colliding with the cross traffic. Sydney inched her way into the intersection, causing cars to slam on their brakes and honk. By the time she got onto Highland, Barbara had more than a block on her and was going at least sixty along the parkway.

Sydney did her best to catch up, but Barbara was taking risks at every intersection. But the cross traffic on Wilshire was heavy and Barbara wasn't able to force her way through, so she turned right, heading west. Sydney followed, noticing Barbara sideswipe a cab before speeding away. Sydney was barely able to get past the resulting jam of vehicles.

Barbara was blaring her horn, trying to force her way through the dense traffic. In front of the Los Angeles County Art Museum a bus pulled out from the curb. Barbara tried to swing around and pass it on the right, but in doing so, she ran into the back of another parked bus. The collision wasn't terrible, but her car was disabled.

Sydney was a few cars behind and, by the time she managed to get to the curb, Barbara had jumped from her car and was running down the sidewalk. Sydney hurried out of the Jaguar and followed in pursuit, pulling her HK from the waistband of her jeans. As she made it to the sidewalk, she saw Barbara round the corner at the cross street. The sound of sirens blared somewhere behind them, perhaps a block or two away.

The redhead was moving briskly. By the time Sydney reached the corner, Barbara had gone forty or fifty yards along the sidewalk of the cross street. It was bordered by the wrought-iron fence surrounding the museum, affording no place to hide.

As she ran, Barbara looked over her shoulder, well aware she was being pursued. Sydney went as fast as she could, noticing for the first time the soreness in her hip. Still, she was rapidly gaining on the madwoman.

Behind the museum was Hancock Park, a flat expanse of lawn speckled with shade trees. Once she'd gotten beyond the fence, Barbara dashed from the sidewalk into the park. There were very few people around, so Barbara was easy to spot. Sydney continued after her, eventually closing to within ten yards. "Stop!" she called to the woman. "Stop! I'm armed!"

Barbara was clearly tiring, as her pace had slowed considerably. Sydney was breathing heavily, even though she was a runner and in pretty good shape.

Suddenly, unexpectedly, the woman stopped and spun around. Sydney came to a halt several yards away. Barbara's chest was heaving and she had a crazed look in her eyes. Sydney pointed her gun at her. "You're under arrest, Barbara," she said between breaths. "It's all over."

"You don't deserve him!" the redhead screamed. "You don't deserve him!"

"Calm down, Barbara," Sydney replied. "We'll get you help."

The woman's expression was devoid of reason. She kept babbling and cursing, then started moving slowly toward Sydney. "You can't have him! I'll kill you first!"

Sydney leveled the muzzle of the weapon at her. "Stop or I'll shoot."

Barbara kept advancing, seemingly indifferent to the threat. Sydney started backing off, to keep some distance between them. She didn't want to fire, but the woman seemed undeterred.

"I'm warning you. I'll shoot!"

The redhead acted as if she was completely oblivious to the danger. There was menace and wild rage in her eyes. She continued to stagger forward, bent, it seemed, on getting to Sydney.

Only a few feet separated them now and Sydney saw that she would either have to shoot her or find another way to subdue her. Then Barbara lunged, and Sydney tried to strike her with her pistol, but the woman deflected the blow with her arm. She got one hand on Sydney's throat, the other on her gun hand. In the ensuing struggle, the weapon went flying away.

Barbara was shrieking hysterically now, clawing at her. Sydney managed to grab a handful of red hair and wrench her head back. That gave her the opportunity to duck under Barbara's arm and throw her over her shoulder. The woman landed on the grass with a thud, the wind knocked out of her.

Sydney quickly pounced, rolling her onto her stomach and pinning her arms behind her. Barbara was weeping now, between gasps. Sydney felt the adrenaline surging through her blood. She pressed her knee firmly into the woman's back to keep her subdued. As she looked around to find someone to summon help, she saw a couple of uniformed police officers running in her direction. One was a thin blond man, the other a stockily-built black woman.

Arriving first at the scene, the female officer removed a pair of handcuffs from her utility belt and got down next to Barbara, easing Sydney aside as she applied the cuffs. Their captive was babbling and weeping—emotionally hysterical, but physically spent.

The officer, perspiration running down the side of her face, looked up at Sydney. "You the P.I., Charles?"

Sydney nodded. "Yeah."

The other cop had retrieved Sydney's gun from the grass. "This yours or hers?"

"Mine."

He sniffed the muzzle to see if it had been fired. "I'll hang on to it for the time being."

The female officer stood, glancing down at the sobbing woman on the ground, then at Sydney. "Good work."

"She belongs in a hospital," Sydney said.

"Yeah, I guess," the female cop replied. "One with a padded cell, by the looks of it." She shook her head. "You all right?"

"I'm fine."

"Need anything?"

"Just to go home and smell my roses."

"Huh?"

"My— A friend sent me some flowers this morning, just before I came after her," Sydney explained, gesturing toward Barbara.

The female officer grinned, showing her large white teeth. "Sounds like you've had quite a day, and it's not even lunchtime."

Sydney ran her fingers back through her half-dried hair. "Yeah. No telling what will happen this afternoon." She tried to remember if Zinn had said when he'd be getting in. She couldn't recall. But one thing was certain—she was definitely looking forward to seeing him.

SYDNEY WASN'T ABLE TO leave for over an hour. After the ambulance took Barbara Walsh off to the hospital, Sydney had to help the police with their reports. Marvin Kaslow arrived at the park and talked to her for a while. The press, including a TV news crew, showed up. Sydney spoke to the reporter on camera, then went over to Kaslow to ask if she could go home.

"Looks like you're a regular hero," the detective said wryly.

"It would be *heroine*, Marvin. But I'm not so sure what I did was all that special. I'm just glad I didn't have to shoot her."

"You're going to be the town's most famous P.I., kiddo. The cases will come flooding in, that's for sure. Garrett's going to be pleased. Maybe he'll even give you a bonus." Kaslow grinned.

"Speaking of Zinn, would you mind letting him know Barbara's in custody? He'll be anxious to hear what's happened."

"What about you?"

"I'm sure I'll be talking to him later. Right now I just want to go home, get cleaned up and lie down."

Kaslow slapped her on the back. "I'll take care of it."

Sydney made her way to Zinn's Jaguar, which the police had moved around to Sixth Street, behind the park. The drive to Glendale at an ordinary speed seemed bizarre after several days of living at double time. Zinn's comment about their need to see each other under normal conditions stuck in her mind. It would be interesting to see what that was like.

When Sydney got to her mother's place and told her what had happened, Lee dropped into a chair, fanning herself with her hand.

"Dear Lord!" she said, looking down at Sydney's grass-stained T-shirt and jeans.

"Well, it's over, Mother. Look at it that way."

Lee rolled her eyes. "Sydney, if something serious had happened to you, I'd have killed you, truly I would."

Sydney dropped onto the sofa, physically and emotionally exhausted.

"Honestly," Lee went on, "if I'd wanted this kind of excitement, I'd have had a son."

Sydney grinned. "This way, you sort of get both."

They looked at each other, then laughed. "You know," Lee said, "I don't know why I'm telling you this, but I believe your father, had he lived, would have been proud of you. It's just a hunch, but I think it's true. Dick always valued eccentricity. I suspect that was a problem between us. I was actually terribly conventional in most respects, though people never would have known it."

Sydney smiled ruefully. "I wish Zinn valued eccentricity."

"Oh!" Lee exclaimed. "Zinn! I completely forgot. He called half an hour ago. Wanted me to tell you his director was keeping them over in San Francisco for another night. Something had gone wrong with last night's shoot and they had to redo a couple of scenes. He said he'd be back tomorrow afternoon, in time to pick you up for the premiere. He said he'd be here by six." Lee got up from her chair and stepped over to the sofa to sit beside Sydney. "I hope you don't mind, but I told him that you loved the flowers and were deeply touched."

Sydney shrugged. "I don't mind. As a matter of fact, it's true."

"I also told him you were terribly eager to see him...."

Sydney looked at Lee with suspicion. "What else did you tell him?"

"That all you did was talk about him. That you adored his daughter. That—"

Sydney held up her hand. "I think I've heard enough."

"I was being truthful," Lee said. "I know you better than you realize, Sydney. Isn't everything I just said true?"

She knew there was no point in arguing. "Thank goodness the days of the arranged marriage are over."

Lee frowned. "Unfortunately, he didn't bring up the subject of marriage."

Sydney rolled her eyes. "Well, I'm going to get cleaned up. If Zinn should call while I'm in the shower, try not to tell him we've been shopping for wedding dresses."

"Then you *are* thinking in those terms!"

Sydney had gone to the entrance to the hallway where she stopped and turned around. "Mom, I love you, but you want to know something? You're a Trojan horse."

"What do you mean by that?"

"I mean I'm not going to discuss Zinn with you anymore," she replied as she disappeared down the hall. "I'm no match for you. I've finally discovered that." Behind her, she could hear Lee laughing with glee.

10

ZINN SAT UNDER THE umbrella by the pool, sipping a glass of iced tea. He was in his tuxedo, waiting for the limousine to arrive. After he'd gotten home a couple hours earlier he'd called Glendale, but Lee had told him that Sydney was at the hairdresser's.

It seemed bizarre to think he was picking her up to take her to a premiere, when all he really wanted to do was be alone with her. But they'd slipped into the mind-set of the occasion, and their first time together since San Francisco would, by force of circumstances, be a date.

He'd talked to her just once since Barbara had been taken into custody. The previous night, while the crew was having dinner at Scott's Seafood Bar and Grill on Lombard, he had slipped out to telephone her and express his appreciation for what she'd done.

Sydney had been a little wistful during the conversation—almost shy—but had admitted she was looking forward to seeing him. Even though the original purpose of going to the premiere was no longer valid, she said there was no point in leaving him without a date at the eleventh hour.

Zinn had flown back to L.A., not quite sure what to make of the situation. His feelings for Sydney Charles weren't so much at issue as his doubts about her attitude toward him. Whether she had come to accept him as an individual or not, she still had misgivings about his work. And she was adamant about her own life-style and career. What he didn't know was whether that rendered them incompatible over the long haul. She was right about one thing—great sex and strong mutual attraction weren't enough.

"Daddy! How come you're out here?" It was Andrea, a teddy bear in her arm, walking out to the pool.

Zinn held out his arms to her and she ran and jumped on his lap. He gave her a big kiss. "I'm just relaxing before I have to go."

"What's 'relaxing'?"

He laughed and pinched her nose. "Daddy really missed you, angel face."

"I missed you, too." She hugged her teddy bear as he hugged her.

Zinn ran his fingers over her wet braid. He'd taken a few minutes to swim with her after he'd gotten home and, while he'd dressed, Yolanda had helped her change, and braided her hair. The housekeeper had told him that Andrea refused to have her hair any other way. "Always like Sydney's," the woman had said. "You would think she is the girl's own mother."

"Can I come to the party with you and Sydney?" Andrea asked.

"I wish you could, honey, but it's only for big people. Daddy will be home when you get up in the morning, though. Don't worry."

"Will Sydney be home, too?"

"I wish she would, but I don't know."

"I want her to come back."

"I'll tell her that."

Zinn had thought more than once how nice it was that the two of them were so fond of each other. Andrea's relationship with the women in his life had always been a concern, but he'd tried not to let it influence him unduly. It was a bonus if the woman he loved also loved his daughter, but it could never be a primary consideration. And yet children, money, careers—those were the things that broke relationships if the differences were too great. He liked it that Sydney was so fond of his child.

"Señor Garrett!" Yolanda called from the house. "The limousine, it is here!"

Zinn walked back inside, holding Andrea's hand. She went with him to the front door, asking him to kiss her teddy bear goodbye as well as her, which he did. She beamed. "And kiss Sydney, too," she said.

"Angel, that's something I'll definitely do."

SYDNEY, DRESSED AND READY, was standing in front of the full-length mirror in her room when she heard the doorbell ring. Knowing Zinn had arrived, her heart gave a little leap. She turned her body to get a good look at the dress she'd come to adore. It was made of heavy duchess satin in an ivory shade. The skirt was full, the neck high. It had long sleeves and a very low back. With her hair pulled into an intricate, low chignon, she looked very elegant indeed.

Eight years earlier she'd stood on that very spot in her prom dress, waiting for her date to arrive. How much and how little had changed.

Lee came to get her. Sydney took a last look at what Zinn would see, then followed her beaming mother to the front room.

He was standing by the window, next to Lee's roses. He was in a black double-breasted tuxedo with the traditional wide bow tie. He looked devastatingly handsome. One hand rested casually in his pants pocket, and his body was turned slightly. When she appeared, his gaze moved up and down her, taking her in, and a smile of delight slowly crept across his face.

For several moments they looked at each other, then Lee asked, "Isn't she beautiful?"

"Extraordinarily," Zinn replied. He stepped over to her, taking her hand and kissing it. Then he brushed his cheek against hers, inhaling her fragrance.

Sydney shivered.

"I'm almost afraid to touch you," he said.

"I won't break," she said with a laugh. "Not after yesterday."

Zinn smiled. Then he slipped an arm around her waist and turned her toward Lee. "Will we do?" he asked.

Lee looked spellbound. Her hands were clasped together over her breast. "You are the most beautiful couple I've ever seen! And believe me, I've seen a lot in Hollywood."

"At least you're objective, Mother," Sydney teased, poking her tongue in her cheek.

Zinn gave her a squeeze. "Come on, Syd, no cynicism. Personally, I think she's right." He grinned at her.

They went out to the waiting limo then, after Lee kissed them both goodbye. When they were settled comfortably into the back seat, Zinn took her hand.

"Andrea asked me to give you a kiss," he said. "She misses you."

"I miss her, too."

"May I, then?"

"Of course."

Zinn leaned over and kissed her gently on the lips. His mouth hovered near hers for a moment, before he leaned back in his seat. For some reason, despite their past intimacy, Sydney was as nervous as a schoolgirl on her first date.

Zinn seemed to sense her trepidation and took her hand. He was quiet, seemingly content just to be with her.

"It's almost strange not to have to worry about Barbara anymore, isn't it?" Sydney asked.

"Yes. Every once in a while I have to stop and tell myself it's really over, that I can relax." He rubbed her hand with his thumb as she looked out the window. They were on the freeway.

Sydney tried not to look at him, because if she did— if she really looked at him—she knew she'd wilt. Zinn was holding back, which was a kindness in a way, but at the same time it made her more nervous.

"Kaslow told me you were a regular heroine, Syd. I'm proud of you, as well as grateful."

She couldn't resist looking at him then. "Are you really?"

"Of course. You've dedicated yourself to your work and I'm happy for you that you've done so well."

"It could help my career," she added, watching his face closely. "Publicity is important in my business, just like it is in yours."

"If anybody ever asks me for a recommendation, I'll give you the very best."

She wanted to ask him if that was really how he felt, but she didn't know what words to use. And she was afraid to do anything to ruin their evening. Yet, at the same time, she knew that the most important thing to do was for them to communicate their needs and feelings openly.

Before long they were on Hollywood Boulevard. The traffic was heavy. Every other vehicle seemed to be a limousine. The windows of most were darkened—celebrities, moving anonymously through the streets. In spite of the way she was dressed, Sydney felt out of place, much like the way she'd felt as a child when her mother dragged her to a studio for a casting call.

Finally the chauffeur pulled up at the end of a long queue of limos lined up at the entrance to the theater, a block ahead. Sydney realized that she wasn't happy. It wasn't that she was afraid; she simply felt uncomfortable. She wanted to be with Zinn, but not in a Hollywood setting. She didn't want pretense and fantasy; she wanted the reality of loving and knowing she was loved in return. She glanced at Zinn. He looked serene.

"Have you been looking forward to tonight?" she asked.

"Not really, if you want to know the truth. All I've really been looking forward to was being with you."

She blushed and squeezed his hand. The limo inched ahead, moving closer to the entrance of the theater.

"You aren't enjoying this, are you?" Zinn asked.

"Of course, I am," she protested.

"No, you're not. I can tell."

"Zinn, how many private investigators get to go to a movie premiere as the guest of a star?"

He searched her eyes. "Somehow that doesn't ring true."

Sydney swallowed hard before she spoke. "It's part of your life and I'm flattered that you wanted me to attend with you, even if it started out as part of our plan to catch Barbara."

The limo continued to inch ahead. They were less than a block from the theater now. There were about half a dozen vehicles in front of them when Zinn leaned forward and tapped on the glass separating them from the driver. The man opened the little window by his ear.

"Pull out of line, Eddie," he said. "I've changed plans."

"Where to, Mr. Garrett?"

"I don't know. Drive around. Go out Santa Monica Boulevard toward the beach, and I'll decide."

"Zinn," Sydney demanded, "what are you doing?"

"I suddenly lost my appetite for the premiere. I don't think Mike will miss us."

She looked back at the line of limos. "But we're here."

"Are you dying to go and be seen?"

Reluctantly, she answered, "No, not really."

"I'm not, either. I'm more in the mood for an omelet or something. Ever eaten at Norm's?"

"Well, sure. Everyone has. There's one not too far from my mother's."

"Let's drive around until we find one, then."

Sydney couldn't quite believe it. She glanced at the theater as they drove by. Crowds had gathered to see the celebrities getting out of their limos, photographers were snapping pictures. Beautiful women wearing plastic smiles were being escorted to the entrance. Sydney was surprised at the relief she felt. She turned to Zinn, who'd leaned back in the seat, appearing perfectly content.

"Did you do this because of me?" she asked.

"I did it because of us."

"I hope I didn't say anything that—"

"Sydney, this is what I want."

"Are you sure?"

Zinn took both her hands in his. "Syd, in that dress you're the most beautiful thing I've ever seen. If it's not important to you that the rest of the world sees you, I'm certainly happy to keep you all to myself."

Before long they found a Norm's and Zinn had the chauffeur park in front. As he helped Sydney out, cars passing on the boulevard honked. A family with two small kids who'd been walking along the sidewalk stopped to stare. People seated by the window inside the restaurant peered out at them. Sydney took Zinn's arm and they followed the family up the walk to the entrance.

"Do you suppose I'm the first guy on a prom date to take his girl to Norm's for dinner?" he asked out of the side of his mouth.

"Probably," she replied with a happy laugh.

Inside, the hostess stared at them, round-eyed. Mechanically taking two menus from the stand as she gazed at Zinn, she said, "Smoking or nonsmoking, Mr. Adams?"

"Thanks, but I believe these people were ahead of us," he said, gesturing toward the family.

The hostess turned red. "Uh, sorry." She led the family away, returning after a moment to escort them to a booth in the corner. People at the counter swiveled on their seats as Sydney went past in her long ivory gown. Other customers murmured comments of surprise. One little old woman with blue hair said, "Wasn't she a Charlie's Angel?"

A waitress, whose nameplate identified her as Marge, brought them glasses of water. Sydney looked up at the woman in her brown-and-beige uniform and matching cap.

"Evening," the woman said, smiling, though she was trying to be blasé. "Can I bring you anything to drink?"

"I'd liked iced tea," Sydney told her.

"Make it two," Zinn added. "Are we agreed on omelets?" he asked Sydney.

"Sure. You're the expert."

"We'll order now," he said to the woman.

There was a list of ingredients the customer could select from and Zinn picked about half of the items that were available. Sydney was a little more modest, choosing only mushrooms and cheese.

The waitress went away and they chatted for a while under the watchful eyes of half the customers in the restaurant. Two older women and a girl of about eight were the only ones who disturbed them for autographs—both Zinn's and Sydney's.

"What show are you on?" the girl asked Sydney.

"*Mission Impossible*," she replied with a wink at Zinn. And when the child screwed up her face in perplexity, Sydney explained that it was a bad joke.

They were able to eat in peace, and Sydney actually relaxed enough to enjoy herself. Zinn seemed to be having a good time, too. She found herself looking into his hazel-green eyes and forgetting to keep her emotions in check. Despite the way they were dressed and the attention they were getting, she kept seeing him as the man she'd been with during their dream night together in San Francisco.

After they'd finished, Zinn had the chauffeur drive them to the beach in Santa Monica. The sun was setting as they got out and walked along the palm-lined park bordering the beach. Joggers, people on skates and bikes, gawked at the strangely dressed pair, but mainly they were left undisturbed.

The air was pleasant and Sydney took Zinn's arm as they strolled. He caught a passing Frisbee once and, laughing, tossed it back to the fellow chasing it.

"Just think," he said, as the sun dipped below the horizon out over the Pacific, "if Lloyd Ferris hadn't come to the law school that day, you might be walking along here with a lawyer."

"More likely, you'd be walking with somebody else," she replied.

"I don't believe that. Somehow, somewhere, we were destined to meet, Sydney."

She smiled at him, appreciating the sentiment. But her calculating side, as her mother called it, couldn't accept that. "That's a romantic notion."

"What's wrong with that?"

"Nothing's *wrong* with it. It's just that I think we have a more fundamental problem."

"Such as?"

They left the walkway and strolled across the grass toward the low wall that ran along the edge of the cliff. Below them was the beach—a broad stretch of sand that was nearly deserted at twilight. Farther to the south the twinkling lights of the Santa Monica pier jutted out into the water. She glanced at him. He was waiting for her answer.

"Well?" he prompted. "What's our problem?"

Sydney put her head on his shoulder as the soft ocean breeze wafted over them. "I'm not sure we share the same world. I guess I'm afraid to believe we do."

"We aren't the same, and it would be terrible if we were. Isn't the real question if we can accept each other as we are?"

She was relieved just to hear him say it. "Yes, that's what I've worried about."

"Then there's no problem."

"You must have some doubts of your own, Zinn."

He stared out to sea. The vibrant colors of the sunset played on his skin. He seemed to be struggling to find the words. "If I've had a concern, it's over what you really want in life."

"What do you mean?"

"You know . . . Your priorities—what's important to you."

"Zinn, I'm not Monica, if that's what worries you."

He turned to her, his eyes shimmering. "I know you have to do what you really want. If I couldn't accept that, you'd be unhappy. I tried to be tolerant of Monica's ambitions. It wasn't fair to deny her anything, and yet, Andrea and I just weren't as important to her as other things. I guess, to be honest, when you insisted on going after Barbara with single-mindedness, I had a feeling of déjà vu. That's what worried me. Not that I didn't want you to do your thing. But . . ."

"I understand that, Zinn. I guess what comes first depends on the circumstances. In each situation that comes along, choices have to be made. Monica made her choice by leaving. I wouldn't have done that."

He contemplated her for a long time. Then he gently pulled her to him and kissed her. When their lips parted, she looked up into his eyes. He had a serenity about him. He seemed relaxed, even confident. He ran his hand up and down her bare back.

"Sydney, this might sound abrupt, but I know very clearly what I want now. The future—the problems it will bring—is never certain, but if we're committed to each other, we can solve it all. I want you to marry me. I want you to be my wife."

He put his hand to her cheek and looked into her eyes adoringly. She felt emotions well within her. "Zinn . . . I . . ."

"I know it's sudden, but I don't want you to mistake my motives, either. I'm aware of what you think of my world, my work. But I think you also see how I've tried to keep my personal life sane and normal. That's the life I want to share with you."

"Oh, Zinn . . ."

She put her arms round him and hugged him, pressing her face into the crook of his neck. Before she knew it, she was crying, with tears running down her cheeks.

He pulled back from her and looked into her eyes. She was trying to stop crying, but couldn't.

"Sydney, darling, I've been an actor for most of my working life, and I think I know people, but I'll be damned if I can tell if that's yes or no."

She laughed through her tears, wiping her eyes. "It's yes! Doesn't Grant Adams always get the girl?"

He stroked her head. "Yes. But he's not used to the girl getting him."

"Zinn, this is Hollywood. *Anything* can happen."

JAYNE ANN KRENTZ

A two-part epic tale from one of today's most popular romance novelists!

Dreams
Parts One & Two

The warrior died at her feet, his blood running out of the cave entrance and mingling with the waterfall. With his last breath he cursed the woman— told her that her spirit would remain chained in the cave forever until a child was created and born there....

So goes the ancient legend of the Chained Lady and the curse that bound her throughout the ages—until destiny brought Diana Prentice and Colby Savager together under the influence of forces beyond their understanding. Suddenly they were both haunted by dreams that linked past and present, while their waking hours were filled with danger. Only when Colby, Diana's modern-day warrior, learned to love, could those dark forces be vanquished. Only then could Diana set the Chained Lady free....

Available in September wherever Harlequin books are sold.

JK92

Take 4 bestselling love stories FREE

Plus get a FREE surprise gift!

WELCOME TO

The quintessential small town, where everyone knows everybody else!

Finally, books that capture the pleasure of tuning in to your favorite TV show!

GREAT READING...GREAT SAVINGS...AND A FABULOUS FREE GIFT!

Each book set in Tyler is a self-contained love story; together, the twelve novels stitch the fabric of the community. The covers honor the old American tradition of quilting; each cover depicts a patch of the large Tyler quilt.

With Tyler you can receive a fabulous gift, ABSOLUTELY FREE, by collecting proofs-of-purchase found in each Tyler book. And use our special Tyler coupons to save on your next TYLER book purchase.

Join your friends at Tyler for the seventh book, ARROWPOINT by Suzanne Ellison, available in September.

Rumors fly about the death at the old lodge! What happens when Renata Meyer finds an ancient Indian sitting cross-legged on her lawn?

HARLEQUIN®

Temptation®

the Fortune Boys

A funny, sexy miniseries from bestselling
author Elise Title!

**LOSING THEIR HEARTS MEANT
LOSING THEIR FORTUNES...**
If any of the four Fortune brothers were unfortunate
enough to wed, they'd be permanently divorced from
the Fortune millions—thanks to their father's last will
and testament.

**BUT CUPID HAD OTHER PLANS FOR
DENVER'S MOST ELIGIBLE BACHELORS!**
Meet Adam in #412 **ADAM & EVE** (Sept. 1992)
Meet Peter in #416 **FOR THE LOVE OF PETE**
  (Oct. 1992)
Meet Truman in #420 **TRUE LOVE** (Nov. 1992)
Meet Taylor in #424 **TAYLOR MADE** (Dec. 1992)

**WATCH THESE FOUR MEN TRY TO WIN AT
LOVE AND NOT FORFEIT $$$**

HARLEQUIN®

Temptation®

COMING NEXT MONTH